"Would you like to dance?" Eli asked.

"Go ahead, Mommy," Opal said before Jamie could get her mouth open. "Rose and I already danced with Mr. Payton. It's your turn."

Something in the way Eli's gaze rested on her face made her feel he wasn't asking because it was her turn. She took a breath to calm the flip-flop in her stomach. "I'd love to."

The smile he gave her in return undid any calm her cleansing breath had achieved. He walked around the table and took her hand. When they reached the makeshift dance floor, he placed his other hand on the small of her back and glided into the song with his usual athletic grace.

"Hey." Eli's breath caressed her hair. "I didn't step on your foot, did I?"

"No." She relaxed and let him lead her in flow with the music. "You're a great dancer."

He laughed, soft and low, strumming a chord deep inside her.

Books by Jean C. Gordon

Love Inspired

Small-Town Sweethearts
Small-Town Dad
Small-Town Mom

JEAN C. GORDON's

writing is a natural extension of her love of reading. From that day in first grade when she realized *t-h-e* was the word *the,* she's been reading everything she can put her hands on. A professional financial planner and editor for a financial publisher, Jean is as at home writing retirement and investment-planning advice as she is writing romance novels, but finds novels a lot more fun.

She and her college-sweetheart husband tried the city life in Los Angeles, but quickly returned home to their native upstate New York. They share a 170-year-old farmhouse just south of Albany, New York, with their daughter and son-in-law, two grandchildren and a menagerie of pets. Their son lives nearby. While Jean creates stories, her family grows organic fruits and vegetables and tends the livestock du jour.

Although her day job, writing and family don't leave her a lot of spare time, Jean likes to give back when she can. She and her husband team-taught a seventh-and-eighth-grade Sunday school class for several years. Now she shares her love of books with others by volunteering at her church's Book Nook.

You can keep in touch with her at www.Facebook.com/JeanCGordon.Author, www.JeanCGordon.com or write her at P.O. Box 113, Selkirk, NY 12158.

Small-Town Mom

Jean C. Gordon

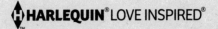

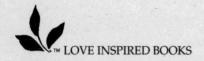

™ LOVE INSPIRED BOOKS

ISBN-13: 978-0-373-81706-1

SMALL-TOWN MOM

Copyright © 2013 by Jean Chelikowsky Gordon

www.LoveInspiredBooks.com

Printed in U.S.A.

So be strong and courageous! Do not be afraid and
do not panic before them. For the Lord your God
will personally go ahead of you.
He will neither fail you nor abandon you.

—*Deuteronomy* 31:6

To all of our men and women in uniform
past and present, with a special thanks
to my critique partners Chris D'Allaird,
former U.S. Army, and Bonnie Hazard,
who connected me with her brother currently
serving in the army, and to my brother-in-law,
former air force captain Wallace F. Gordon.

Chapter One

Not again.

Not when she'd finally gotten her family through the worst. It had been a rough eighteen months. But Jamie Glasser thought her son, Myles, was on track and life back to normal. As normal as could be under the circumstances.

She replayed the voice mail message as she pulled her crossover SUV into the Schroon Lake Central School parking lot and steeled herself to meet the new guidance counselor.

She got out and slammed the vehicle door shut. The guidance counselor's curt summons had put her on edge almost as much as imagining what Myles had done to prompt the call.

"Jamie," Thelma Wood, the ageless office manager, greeted her as she entered the K-12 school's main office to sign in. The older woman's cool tone clearly said she hadn't gotten over her displeasure with Jamie having given up her position as school nurse to join the midwife practice at the Ticonderoga birthing center.

"Thelma." Jamie wrote her name, the time and her in-school destination on the clipboard on the counter separating Thelma's business domain from students, parents and the rest of the general public.

"I expect you're here to see our Mr. Payton."

Our Mr. Payton. The new guidance counselor must be really something to have Mrs. Woods claiming him as her own after being on the job only a month.

"He and Myles are in the guidance office."

Myles? The phone message hadn't said that the guidance counselor had kept Myles after school. That meant he wouldn't be there with the girls when the bus dropped them off.

Jamie turned the clipboard so that Mrs. Woods could read the sheet, left the office and pulled out her cell phone.

"Hello," her friend Emily Stacey answered on the second ring.

"Hi, it's Jamie." She hesitated for a moment. Since she'd lost her faith and dropped out of the Singles Plus group and everything else connected with Hazardtown Community Church after her husband was killed in Afghanistan, Jamie hadn't seen much of Emily. But Emily was the only person she could think of who would be home. "Any chance you could run over and meet the girls' bus?"

"Sure. Is everything okay?"

"Myles is in some kind of trouble—again. So he won't be at the house when they get off the bus."

"I'm sorry. Any problem with my bringing them over here?"

"Not at all." Gratitude flushed away the guilt Jamie harbored about neglecting their friendship these past few months. "Thanks so much."

"Not a problem. You'd do the same. Good luck with Myles."

Considering some of her son's antics last year, she might need it. "I'll come get the girls as soon as I can."

"Whenever. I'm planning on putting them to work entertaining Isabelle and Ryan so I can finish an ad mock-up I need to get out to a client today."

"Good plan. See you soon." *I hope.*

Jamie hung up and headed down the familiar hall. The knot in her stomach tightened with each step. She slowed her pace as she neared the guidance office, postponing the meeting as long as she could.

After a trying school year, where Myles seemed to be in some kind of trouble every other week, he'd had a good summer as a junior counselor at Camp Sonrise on nearby Paradox Lake, where she'd been the camp nurse the three previous summers. Before she'd had to take a better-paying, year-round job at the birthing center. Jamie had been a little jealous of Myles. She'd really liked being with the kids at Sonrise full-time during the summer months.

The guidance office door was ajar. Jamie paused. She couldn't go through another school year like last year. Taking a deep breath, she pushed the door open to see Myles sitting in front of the guidance counselor's desk with his back to her.

"Mrs. Glasser?" The man seated at the desk didn't wait for her to answer. "Please come in and sit down."

She shot Myles a look before turning her attention to the counselor. His strong-featured masculine good looks at least partly explained fussy Mrs. Woods's warming to him so quickly.

His glance at the wall clock and the fleeting frown that marred his ruggedly handsome face muted any welcome in his deep voice and polite words.

"I'm Eli Payton." He rose in a smooth, controlled manner and offered her his hand.

Something in the way Eli moved and spoke— his brisk handshake and curt phone message— reminded Jamie of her late husband, John. She gave Eli a quick once-over. The high and tight hair. The way his off-the-rack suit hung on his fit figure as if it were tailored especially for him. His clean, neat desktop devoid of any unnecessary personal items.

After a spark of attraction, bile burned the back of her throat.

Eli Payton was a soldier, a career soldier. Someone who wasn't used to being around military personnel might not see it, but Jamie did.

So why was he working as a high school guidance counselor?

She pulled her hand back as soon as he released it and unbuttoned her coat. She slipped her coat onto the back of the chair next to Myles, sensing Eli's eyes on her. What was she doing? She didn't *know* he was former military. She just had a strong feeling he was. And if he were, that wasn't a good reason to dislike him.

As she turned back toward him and took her seat, Eli glanced at the clock again. Jamie rechanneled her irritation. It wasn't her fault that it was well after the close of classes. She wasn't the one who'd called the meeting. If he had somewhere to be, he could have asked her to come in tomorrow morning.

She planted her feet firmly on the floor, her white Crocs squeaking as she pressed them to the polished tiles. And no matter how many times he checked the clock, he wasn't going to make her feel that she was in the wrong because she'd been doing her job and hadn't gotten his phone message until after she and the midwife had finished the delivery. Except she did feel uneasy, and his dismissive perusal of her hospital scrubs didn't help. It wasn't as if she'd had time to go home and change.

"As you know from the incident notice Myles brought home for you to sign yesterday—"

Jamie pinned her gaze on her son who had evidently found something riveting on the floor between his chair and the guidance counselor's desk. "What incident notice?"

Eli raised an eyebrow and pushed an all-too-familiar yellow form across the desk to her. She read down to her signature. Except it wasn't *her* signature.

"I didn't see or sign this." She moved the paper a few inches away from her.

"So I gather," Eli said with a wry smile that would have normally appealed to her sense of humor. But there was nothing humorous about this situation.

"Myles. Seriously? What were you thinking?"

"Aw, Mom. It isn't that big a deal."

"Stealing exam answers and selling them to other kids isn't a big deal? Since when?" Jamie tried to keep the screech out of her voice but failed.

"I didn't steal the answers. I went back into Mrs. Norton's room to get my iPod." He waved his hand at her. "I know. I'm not supposed to take it to school. When I was leaving, there was this paper on the floor."

"The exam answer key was on the floor?" Eli's voice had an edge to it that Jamie wouldn't want used on her. She felt sorry for Becca Norton, Myles's history teacher, if Myles was telling the truth.

"No, it was just a paper. I crumpled it up and shot it across the room at the trash can." Myles grimaced. "I missed, so I went over to toss it in the can and I saw the test in there. It wasn't the final test. It didn't have the answers, and Mrs. Norton had scribbled through the questions. I told you, I didn't steal the answers."

"The answers, the test. Not a lot of difference," Jamie said.

Jamie glanced at Eli to see if Myles's explanation had had any effect on Eli's reaction to Becca throwing out her preliminary test rather than shredding it. The set of his jaw said no.

Her stomach roiled. Jamie felt a kinship with Becca. The woman needed her job. She was a single mother, too. Becca's husband had abandoned her when he'd accepted a promotion and job transfer to his company's home office in Hartford and had taken his secretary—not Becca and their son— with him. Jamie hated that her son's stupid act might jeopardize his teacher's job.

"I took the test and looked up the answers myself and sold them," Myles finished, as if his providing the answers somehow made it right.

At one time Jamie thought her raising Myles and his sisters in a Christian home had provided a better influence on them. John's death in Afghanistan had corrected that misconception. God wasn't there for her or her family.

"What do you think the consequence of your action should be?" Eli asked.

"A week's suspension?" Myles voice rose at the end of the last word.

Eli nodded. "Sounds fair."

Jamie's temperature ticked up. He was going to punish Myles by letting him stay home for a week? "I don't think…" A spark in Eli's steel-blue eyes and twitch of his mouth cooled her temper, if not her temperature.

"In-school suspension. Here in the guidance office, with me." Eli focused on Myles. "You'll do all of your class work and write Mrs. Norton a letter of apology. I'm certain she put a lot of work into developing that test, and she'll need to create a replacement one."

"I guess. Can we go now?"

"Yes. Report to me when you get off the bus on Monday."

"Thank you," Jamie said.

"Doing my job."

Jamie knew better. Babysitting her wayward child was going above and beyond a guidance counselor's duties. For a fleeting moment, she let herself imagine what it would be like to have a commanding man like Eli Payton in Myles's life. In *her* life.

"Feel free to call me any time you want to check

up on Myles. I saw from the notes in Myles's file
that you worked closely with my predecessor, Erin
Ryder."

"Sure. Thanks again." Jamie pulled her coat from
the back of the chair. She had an unsettling feeling
that working closely with Eli Payton would have a
completely different dimension from working with
Erin.

Eli tapped the spine of the file folder against the
palm of his hand. Myles Glasser and his mother
were another example of what an absent father did
to a family. Not that he was faulting Myles's father
for serving his country and making the supreme
sacrifice. But too often, he'd seen what consecutive
deployments did to families, to some of his closest
friends' families. What Eli's father's job as a long-
haul trucker had done to his mother and him and
his sister. He opened his file cabinet and shoved
the folder in.

Seeing how hard it was for some service families,
and the memories of his father's frequent absences
from their Paradox Lake home, had convinced Eli to
put off starting a family until he'd left. One of many
things he and his ex-fiancée had disagreed about.

Family was important. More people needed to
make it a priority. He'd meant what he said to Mrs.
Glasser about working with her to get Myles on
the straight and narrow. It certainly would be no

hardship for him. Myles reminded him of himself at that age, before he'd gotten into more serious trouble. And Myles's mother was pretty in a fresh girl-next-door way. He appreciated that she wasn't model-slim like so many women aspired to be, and liked the way her curly dark hair framed her heart-shaped face. A face that had run the gamut of emotions from annoyance when she'd first entered his office to exasperation when her son explained his transgression to anger when she'd thought he was going to let Myles off with a suspension.

Eli pushed the cabinet door closed. Myles seemed like a good kid who needed a little guidance. The youth group he and Drew Stacey led at Hazardtown Community Church could give him some direction. Eli searched his memory. Had he seen Jamie and her family at church? No, he would have remembered her. Didn't matter. Several of the youth group's members didn't belong to Community. He'd touch base with Jamie after Myles's suspension was over and mention the group to her.

Eli lifted his jacket from the coat tree by the door and switched off the lights. Maybe if someone had given his mother a hand, helped her organize her own and their family life… His thought trailed off unfinished. He could do that for Jamie and Myles. Eli smiled as he pictured the way Jamie had bit her bottom lip when she'd thought he was going to let

Myles get off with a week out of school. Yes, he could give her a hand and enjoy every minute of it.

"Uh, Mom. Aren't you forgetting something?" Myles asked as Jamie flicked the signal to turn onto their road.

"What?"

"Rose and Opal."

Jamie lifted her foot from the brake and straightened the wheel. "Oh, yeah." She'd forgotten about the girls being at Emily's.

"You're not all upset about this, are you? It's no big deal, or else Payton would have done more than suspend me for a week."

"That's Mr. Payton," she corrected him. "And you stole the exam and helped other kids cheat—for money. That is a big deal. You know better. Whatever prompted you to do it?"

He rolled his eyes. "The money."

The force of his words sent a chill through her. She gave Myles a reasonable allowance for helping around the house and yard, and he'd been shoveling snow for several of their neighbors.

"What do you need more money for?"

"You don't want to know."

He was right. Part of her didn't want to know, but she should. She swallowed. "Yes, I do. Talk to me about it."

"Dad's Miata. I'm trying to buy it back from the

Hills. We were going to restore it. Then you had to go and sell it."

"I had to." John's military pension wasn't enough for them to live on, and finances had been tight before she'd left the school to work at the birthing center. She'd fallen behind on the rent-to-buy lease payments on their house and hadn't wanted to upset their family life more by having to move.

"Right. But your new job pays more. So why don't you buy it back?" he challenged her.

Because seeing the car in the garage every day was too painful. And she'd been so mad at John for dying. Selling the car he'd taken such pride in had been cathartic. She couldn't tell Myles that, though.

"There are other things we need more."

Myles clenched his fists. "You have other things you want more. You don't care what I need. Like you didn't need Dad around." His words jumbled together. "But I did. You didn't want him around, so you could be boss of us."

His words sliced into her heart. Her son had no idea how much she'd missed John when he'd been deployed, and how hard it was for her to be the only parent to Myles and the girls.

She gripped the steering wheel and cut a too-sharp turn onto Hazard Cove Road. "Myles! You and I talked about this before. I'm sorry you feel that way, but I always wanted your dad around." *More than you'll ever know.*

She pulled into the driveway of the camp lodge where Emily and her husband lived.

"I am not buying you the Miata." She took a deep breath. "But I won't stop you from buying it as long as you earn the money legally."

He pushed his bottom lip out in a petulant expression at odds with his man-boy face. When had he gotten so old? It seemed she and John had married only a couple of years ago, not more than fifteen.

"Why should I bother without Dad here to help me restore it?" He sniffled and then glared at her as if to rebuff any sympathy she might show him.

The virtual knife he'd plunged into her heart a moment ago sliced the rest of the way through. Myles threw his door open. She'd get through this as she'd gotten through everything else. By herself. Eli Payton's offer to call him anytime she wanted echoed in her head. Jamie mentally shook off his invitation and the engaging smile he'd given her delivering it. They were only words, like John's last words to her that he'd be home at the end of that month. She closed her eyes against the pain. She'd learned a hard lesson not to take anyone's word at face value.

Chapter Two

Jamie pushed the shopping cart across the Grand Union parking lot and clicked the key remote to open the back door of her crossover. One good thing about her sometimes-erratic hours at the birthing center was that she often had time during the day for errands, like grocery shopping, which left her evenings free to be with the kids.

"Hey, Jamie."

Jamie glanced over her shoulder. Clare Thomas waved from across the parking lot, and as Clare walked toward her, Jamie recognized the woman with her. Becca Norton, Myles's history teacher and Clare's sister-in-law. Shouldn't she be at school? Jamie's mouth went dry, and she let the grocery bag she was holding drop to the cargo-area floor. She hoped Becca hadn't been suspended from her position because of Myles.

"Hi," she managed to say as the two women stopped beside her shopping cart.

"We won't keep you," Clare said.

Famous last words.

"I just wanted to tell you how glad I was when Myles said that you'd given him permission to go to youth group with Tanner on Sunday."

Jamie lifted another bag from the cart to hide her anger. She hadn't done any such thing, and Myles shouldn't have lied and said she had.

When she'd been called into work Sunday afternoon for a delivery, Jamie had asked Clare if Myles could come over and hang out with Tanner. The girls had been at a friend's house and Jamie wasn't sure she trusted Myles not to break his grounding if she or his sisters weren't there. And he'd managed to do it anyway. He'd known she wouldn't want him to go to youth group. When she'd stopped taking him and the girls to church and Sunday school, she'd made it very clear to Myles that neither church nor God had anything to offer any of them.

"Does that mean we'll be seeing you back at church?" Clare asked.

Jamie mumbled a noncommittal reply. No need to make Clare the object of her anger. She'd reserve that for Myles.

"I hope you didn't mind that Eli drove Myles home. He's renting a place at the lake and had to go right by your house."

Eli. So *he* was behind this. When she'd texted Clare on Sunday that she was leaving the birthing center and would swing by and pick up Myles, Clare had texted back that she had to go out anyway and would drop Myles off. And he certainly hadn't said anything about Eli bringing him home. Jamie counted to five. She'd deal with Eli later.

"No, that was fine." She'd never told Clare that Myles *couldn't* go to youth group.

Jamie turned to Becca. "I hope Myles's antics didn't get you in trouble with the school."

"No, the principal was decent." Becca hesitated. "I think she feels sorry for me." The woman grimaced.

"I'm glad I ran into you so I could apologize for Myles. Let me know if he gives you any more trouble."

"I will."

Clare looked at her sister-in-law and grinned. "You'll be seeing a lot of more of Becca over the next few months."

"I hope not." Jamie slapped her hand to her mouth. "I didn't mean that the way it sounds. I'm coming down hard on Myles about his behavior. So, I hope I won't be putting in as much time at the guidance office this year." A point she was going to make clear to Mr. Payton.

"No!" Clare laughed. "Not at the school. You'll be seeing Becca at the center. She's expecting."

Becca shot her sister-in-law a quelling look. It

was clear to Jamie that she hadn't been ready to share that news.

"Congratulations." Jamie's heart went out to Becca and her situation. Jamie had gone through her pregnancies with the girls alone. But at least she'd had the expectation that her husband was coming home, had been able to talk and email with him. Becca didn't even have that. Her husband had abandoned her and their young son and, now, the new baby.

"I'm available to talk if you want. One thing I have a lot of practice doing is being a single parent."

"Thanks," Becca said. "I might take you up on that."

"We'd better let you go," Clare said. "Think about coming back to church. We miss you and the kids."

Jamie pasted a smile on her face and waved goodbye. No sense in causing hard feelings by telling Clare she had no desire to rejoin the Community Church fellowship or any church fellowship. It was a waste of time. She'd learned the hard way that the only person or thing she could depend on was herself. Jamie slammed the back door of the vehicle shut and climbed in the driver's seat to head to her next, unplanned stop—the school. More specifically, Eli Payton's office.

Eli hadn't been able to get Jamie Glasser off his mind all week, and the daily one-on-one with Myles hadn't helped. He glanced at the teen, his dark head bent over the history book he was reading. While Eli was sure Myles wouldn't appreciate the observation, he looked a lot like his mother. Granted, a masculine version of his mother.

"All done." Myles slammed the book shut and started drumming his fingers on the student desk Eli had asked maintenance to move into his office Monday morning. The teen's dark-lashed eyes—his mother's eyes—fixed on the clock slowly ticking away the hour remaining in the school day.

"Stop." Eli shot Myles The Look, the one he had honed training airmen at Maxwell Air Force Base.

The teen's fingers stilled.

"Good. I won't have to make you drop and give me twenty."

"You can't do that." Myles's voice wasn't anywhere near as strong as his words.

"Try me." The teen was right. In the months since he'd returned to Paradox Lake, Eli had found—often, the hard way—that the mindset and actions that had served him well in the Air Force didn't translate well to civilian life. But he wasn't alone. Some of the guys in the Air National Guard unit he'd recently joined had said they'd had the same problem after leaving active duty.

The guidance office door swung open, giving Myles a reprieve and excuse to turn away.

Jamie strode in. "Myles, go to the main office and wait for me."

Despite the menace in his mother's voice, Myles turned to Eli for confirmation before he rose to leave.

"Tell Mrs. Woods that I said to wait for your mother in the office."

Jamie pinched her lips together. Eli could sympathize with her frustration, but she should have established control over her son long before he hit high school age.

Jamie placed her hands palms down on the other side of his desk and leaned across. "Where do you get off undermining my authority and encouraging Myles to disobey me? I didn't tell him he could go to youth group. And I certainly didn't give you permission to drive him home."

"Whoa! Please sit, and lower your voice. Classes are still in session."

Eli stood and moved a chair beside the desk. She sat and grasped her purse in her lap. The flush of her anger accented her cheekbones in an attractive, natural way that no amount of makeup, no matter how carefully applied, could have.

"I did not intentionally undermine you," he said. "Mrs. Thomas accepted my offer to drive Myles home. I was dropping off a couple of other kids, too. Since she'd brought Myles, I assumed her okay was enough."

Jamie's grip on her purse relaxed. "Are you telling me that you didn't mention youth group to him on Friday, invite him to the meeting on Sunday?"

Eli had to walk a fine line talking about church activities. He understood why the school had the policy, but he didn't have to like it. "I didn't say anything to Myles about the meeting, even though it could do him a lot of good to get involved."

Her dark-lashed eyes widened.

"He's looking for some direction, guidance, and I think he could find it at youth group or some other organized activity."

"Guidance that I'm not providing him." She gripped her purse again until her knuckles were white.

That was exactly what he thought, but he knew better as a man and an educator to not say that outright. "We've been talking this week, and Myles said that all he does is go to school and watch his sisters after school and weekends when you work. I'm sure—"

"He watches Rose and Opal the two afternoons I'm scheduled in the practice's office and if there's a delivery, not every day after school and weekends."

"If you'd let me finish, I was going to say that I knew Myles was exaggerating. But you must see the inconsistency in your work schedule and how that might affect Myles. He needs consistency, some time to chill, to just hang out with the guys and not be on constant call."

"Hanging out with the guys, the wrong guys, is what got him in trouble in the first place. I'm sure you read all about the trouble he got himself into last school year." She paused and cleared her throat. "Things were going better this year."

Until he started talking with me. Eli tented his fingers and rested his chin on his pointer fingers, waiting for her to say it. Somehow, she'd made him into the enemy. It was the easiest way out, to find someone else to blame. He'd done it himself. Not that he thought she was intentionally to blame—just a little scattered as pretty women often were. Like his mother. But Jamie obviously had her son's best interests at heart.

"Myles ran cross-country this past fall," she said as if to disprove what Eli had said.

"With Tanner Thomas. Myles told me."

One corner of Jamie's mouth quirked down. "He made the team when he was in seventh grade, but he didn't run last school year."

"That's what I'm saying about hanging out with the guys in an organized activity being good for Myles."

She pushed a thick black curl from her forehead. "And how many groups, clubs and sports teams did you belong to when you were in high school?"

He had her here. "None, after I was booted from

the football team junior year for failing grades." *Among other things.* "You wouldn't want to read *my* school record for the last two years of high school. I would have been a lot better off if I had been involved in something."

"My son is not you." She enunciated each word separately.

"No, he's not. But he may be headed down the same road. It's my job to help him make better choices than I did. I don't want to think about where I'd be today if the armed forces hadn't saved me."

Jamie blanched. "Don't get any ideas about the military *saving* Myles. It didn't save Myles's father. It killed him."

His chest tightened. Granted, he hadn't lost a spouse, but he'd lost close friends in the Middle East, including his former fiancée. "I understand how you might feel like that."

Her frown told him that she didn't believe him. But the service hadn't hardened him so much that he couldn't feel some of her pain. He held her gaze with his for a moment. No way could he miss the spark of anger in her coffee-brown eyes.

"Okay," he conceded. "I may not fully understand, but I still have to do what I believe is best for Myles. It's my job."

The bell signaling the end of the school day rang and stopped Jamie from verbally drawing her line between Eli's job as guidance counselor and her job as Myles's mother. And it was for the better. Right now, she couldn't trust herself not to say things she might regret later. How could he understand? Sure, he'd served his country, just like John, and most likely he'd seen comrades fall. But had he lost a spouse? Did he have children? The lack of any family photos in his office seemed to say no.

She rose. "I should go. I want to catch the girls before they get on the bus so they can ride home with Myles and me."

"I'll call their teachers."

Jamie gave Eli the girls' teachers' names reluctantly. It was peevish on her part. She didn't want Eli to be right about anything. But he *was* right. Calling the teachers would be a better way of catching Rose and Opal.

Eli replaced the phone receiver. "Sorry. Both of their classes have been dismissed."

"Thanks. I have time to get Myles and be home before the bus drops the girls off."

"I'll walk you to the office."

Jamie bit her tongue to stop herself from saying the first thing that had come to mind, that she knew her way to the office. Eli was being polite. And she had to admit that he seemed to be doing what he thought was best for her son. She just didn't happen to agree with him.

He opened the door, and they stepped into the

hall and the onslaught of one hundred and fifty high school and middle school students set loose for the day.

Eli took Jamie's elbow and guided her to the side of the rush, raising her awareness of how close the crush of students had pressed her to him.

"Has Myles shown any interest in running track in the spring?" he asked. "Since he's run cross-country, he might want to do long-distance."

Back to that? She sighed. "He hasn't said anything." Not that Myles shared much with her anymore. "I suppose it couldn't hurt if you broached it with him, if he comes in to talk with you."

Eli nodded and held the office door open for her. She couldn't fault his manners.

"Hello, Jamie, Eli." Thelma Woods's voice softened on his name. "If you're looking for Myles, he left with Liam Russell and one of the other seniors after the final bell."

Jamie tensed. If Eli needed another example of her lack of control over her defiant son, Myles had just provided it.

"He was supposed to wait here for his mother." Eli spoke before she could, his voice low and curt.

She warmed at his including her. Maybe they could be in this together, as long as he respected her parental authority.

Thelma gave Eli a little shrug. "He said you told him to wait here until school was over."

"I'd better go while I still have time to get home before the kids," Jamie said.

"Call me if you need to. Anytime," Eli said.

Jamie smiled and ignored Thelma's raised eyebrow. The woman had an overactive imagination when it came to the personal lives of the school staff. Jamie did not need her speculating that anything was going on between her and Eli except Myles.

Jamie hurried down the hall, passing the high school sports trophy case on her way to the main door. She hadn't been into sports much in high school, except for intramural bowling. But her late husband had been cocaptain of their high school wrestling team and a state champion their senior year. Eli might be right about encouraging Myles to join the track team in the spring.

She pushed open the door, and the bitter north wind hit her face with full force. But for the immediate future, the only running Myles might be doing was running for cover from her.

Ten minutes later, Jamie pulled into her driveway seconds ahead of the school bus. She stepped from her crossover and waited while the bus doors opened.

"Mommy!" Seven-year-old Opal jumped down

and skipped over to her while Rose followed at a more dignified nine-year-old pace. Jamie kept her gaze on the door. It closed and the bus engine roared to life, leaving a cloud of diesel fumes as it pulled away.

"Mommy," Opal repeated. "I got a hundred on my spelling test. Can we go in and have some ice cream to celebrate?"

"After dinner."

The little girl's smile dimmed.

"With whipped cream and sprinkles," Jamie added. No need to take her bad day out on the girls.

"All right!" Opal skipped off to the house.

"Myles wasn't on the bus," Rose said before Jamie could ask. "I saw him walk by with Scott and Liam, my friend Katy's brother. Liam has a really loud car. They used to come over all of the time when you were working, but they haven't in a while, not since you told Myles he couldn't have anyone over without your permission when you're at work. He knows I'll tell on him."

Leave it to Rose to have all of the details and to appoint herself to police Myles. She looked down at her daughter. While Jamie appreciated that the possibility of Rose reporting on him had helped stop Myles from disobeying the house rules, she shouldn't put the little girl in that position.

"Come on, Mom." Rose hitched her backpack up on her shoulder and headed into the house.

After a final glance at the fading form of the school bus, Jamie followed her.

"Here you go." Jamie handed Opal and Rose dishes of ice cream with sprinkles and whipped cream. "As soon as you finish, right to your homework."

Mouth full, with whipped cream on her upper lip, Opal nodded her agreement.

"When I get done, can I watch TV?" Rose asked.

"I'll see. It depends on how late it is."

"I can work fast."

"And still do a good job?"

Rose nodded. "Promise."

Jamie smiled at the girls' chatter as she crossed the room to load the dishwasher. She opened the door and lifted a plate from the counter. This was Myles's job. The girls set and cleared the table and he loaded the dishwasher. But, after the blowup they'd had when he'd arrived home just as they were sitting down to eat, his sullen attitude at the dinner table had stretched her patience to the limit. She'd needed him out of her sight for a while, so she'd sent him up to his room to do his homework—without his cell phone.

"Mom, the phone is ringing," Rose said.

Jamie's gaze darted to Myles's phone on the counter before she realized the faint ring was the house phone, not his cell phone, or hers. So it probably wasn't one of the midwives at the birthing center. She released a sigh of relief. She was on call tonight, but leaving the kids and going into work for a delivery that would take hours was the last thing she wanted to do.

As Jamie followed the faint ringing into the living room, her pulse quickened. Could it be Eli calling to check whether Myles made it home? No, that was silly. Why would he call? A teenage boy hitching a ride home with a couple of friends wasn't anything out of the ordinary. More, why would she want him to call? She didn't even like the man.

When she reached the foot of the stairs, the ringing stopped, and she heard the low rumble of Myles's voice. She froze, startled at how much it sounded like John's. Then anger thawed her immobility. Myles had the living room phone. Fists clenched, she looked up the stairwell with resignation. She couldn't let him get away with this. Maybe Eli had been right, that Myles needed a stronger hand than hers. *No!* She could, *would* handle Myles just as she'd handled a hundred other troubles when John was deployed… Now that he was gone.

She bowed her head and closed her eyes. "Dear Lord, I know I'm a good mother. Please help me be a better one, especially for Myles." Then, she caught herself. What was she doing? She shook her head. She knew prayers were useless. John's death had proven that. But old habits die hard. Lifting a foot that seemed to weigh fifty pounds, Jamie dragged herself up the stairs to the inevitable confrontation. Beside her, tail wagging, their golden retriever, Scooby, whined in sympathy.

"Yes, boy, I couldn't agree more."

Chapter Three

Eli had had a bad feeling about the old heating system in his mom's house the last time he'd been over and heard the pipes clanking. His stop by this afternoon to say hello on the way back from working out at the gym in Crown Point had proven him right. The temperature was subzero outside, and he'd found his mother working in her upstairs studio in fifty-degree cold.

He held his breath and opened the air-release valve on the pipe leading to the radiator in the studio. After a couple of gurgles, the hot water flowed soundlessly, bringing heat to the frosty room. The hot water hadn't been circulating in the upstairs baseboard radiators because of air in the pipes, and his mother hadn't even noticed.

He closed the valve and straightened. That should do it for now. But the valve needed to be replaced. Might as well do it while he was here, although he suspected he'd be back frequently to take care of other home maintenance issues. As far as he could tell, nothing had been done to the house since the last time he'd been here on leave. And that had to have been at least five years ago.

"Mom," he called as he tromped downstairs. "I'm going to run to the hardware store in Ticonderoga. Do you need anything while I'm out?"

His mother appeared in the doorway between the kitchen and the dining room. "Hang on a minute. I'll get my purse and come with you. I need a few things from the grocery superstore that I couldn't get at the Grand Union in Schroon Lake." She brushed past him to go to her room.

Eli stifled a groan. It wasn't that he didn't like his mother's company. But every time they went out, she ran into at least five people she knew but hadn't seen "in ages." Inevitably, a short trip stretched into a major time drain. He'd hoped to be back to his place in time to catch the Army-Air Force football game at four o'clock. He checked his watch. He still might make it.

Sharing his down time with someone else was taking some getting used to. In the service, his time was regimented, but generally when he was off duty, he was on his own to do as he pleased. Since he'd been back in Paradox Lake, he'd seemed to have a lot more demands on his free time. His mother number one. It was almost as if she was trying to make up for the time he'd been away and her unintentionally ignoring him as a child when she was off in her creative world. His sister may have had the right idea settling in the Albany area, putting a hundred miles between her family and Mom.

"All set." Mom flashed him a warm smile that made him feel about two feet tall for the unkind thoughts that had gone through his mind.

She hadn't let the house fall into disrepair on purpose. For the most part, he was sure she hadn't noticed. When she was busy painting, she didn't notice much of anything. And the last five years or so, until Grandma's death last year, Mom had spent winters with her in Florida and hadn't used the studio here during the cold months.

"Okay." He opened the door for her. "Do you want me to drop you at the superstore while I go to the hardware?"

"Oh, no. I'll come to the hardware store with you. I don't have anything else planned for this afternoon."

Eli bit the side of his mouth. Mom genuinely liked his company. And it wasn't that he didn't like spending time with her. But he had plans for the afternoon. He released the storm door and let it slam shut behind him.

His mother chatted away the entire twenty-minute drive to Ticonderoga. As he pulled into the hardware store parking lot, he checked the dashboard clock and calculated whether he had enough time to take Mom shopping, get back to her house and install the new valve then get to his place in time for kickoff.

"Leah!" a familiar voice from the past called as Eli pushed the door to the hardware store open for his mother.

Edna Donnelly, his high school English teacher, waved them over to where she was standing at the checkout with Harry Stowe, his high school principal. Eli had to smile. The elderly couple was quite the item. After dating for three years, they were planning an all-out June wedding. Mom had kept him up-to-date by email on all of the Paradox Lake social news.

"Go ahead," he said. "I'll go back and get what I need." Eli waved to Edna and Harry and walked toward the plumbing section. He lifted the valve he wanted from the display hook and turned toward the back of the store at the sound of a door opening. A woman emerged from the Employees Only area. Her gaze locked on his. *Charlie Meade—Russell now.* An unpleasant reminder of his past.

She quickly closed the distance between them. "Eli, I heard you were back."

"It was time to come home."

She wrinkled her nose in distaste.

"I'm surprised you're still around." In high school, Charlie's number one goal was to leave

Paradox Lake. And when his mother kept him up-to-date on Paradox Lake over the years, Charlie wasn't someone she included in her updates.

"Where else would I be?"

Charlie couldn't still be carrying a grudge because he hadn't taken her with him when he left for the service. They hadn't even been dating seriously. And the lies she'd spread about him afterward… He shook his head.

She glared at him. Evidently, she was still carrying that grudge.

"I've got to get back to work." She turned on her heel and disappeared around the end-cap.

When Eli approached the checkout, Edna, Harry and his mother were still chatting, along with someone else blocked from his view by Harry and the magazine display.

"JR." His mother used his childhood nickname, short for junior. The other woman turned, and his gaze locked with the warm brown eyes that had haunted him the past week in the guise of her son, Myles.

"Here's someone I want you to meet," she said.

"Eli." Jamie's greeting was tentative.

"Hello. Nice to see you again."

Her eyes reflected the question he'd heard in her voice, as if she thought he was simply being polite. He didn't do simply polite. It was nice seeing her. He enjoyed running into his students' parents around town. It lent another dimension to working with the kids. Had his meetings with Jamie left her with that bad of an impression of him? He kind of liked her, and they needed to have at least a cordial relationship if they were going to work together for Myles's benefit. Eli dismissed the flicker of concern in his gut. He'd only been doing his job.

"You know each other," his mother said.

"Yes, he's Myles's guidance counselor." Jamie ran her gaze over the tall commanding man standing next to the diminutive Leah and swallowed to extinguish the flash of attraction that flared. "I had no idea your son, JR, was Eli."

Leah had been her daughter Opal's preschool Sunday school teacher, and she'd often talked with Jamie about her son in the Air Force and his early tours in the Middle East as a helicopter pilot. Family in the military had been something they'd had in common when they'd first met. But the nickname, the fact that Leah's last name was Summers, not Payton… Jamie hadn't made the connection between them. And she'd stopped going to church long before Eli had returned to Paradox Lake.

Leah laughed. "That's right. You've only been here a few years. You wouldn't know he's JR or that I kept my maiden name."

"I'd never do that," Edna said, resting her gaze

fondly on her octogenarian fiancé. "But I know a lot of my students have."

"I thought I was such a radical back then."

Leah's pensive look made Jamie wonder if Leah had regrets, or if she was simply remembering a younger time when she'd made that "radical" decision. A time when she had a doting man like Edna did now. Now that some of her pain had dulled, Jamie found her thoughts going back in time more often.

"I hate to cut our visit short," Edna said. "We have to get going. Harry wants to watch the Army-Air Force game at four. West Point is his alma mater."

"Yeah, I want to catch it, too," Eli said, checking his watch. "But you know I'll be rooting for the Falcons."

Harry chuckled as he took Edna's arm. "May the better team win. And we all know which one that is." He escorted the older woman to the door.

Eli stepped to the right of Jamie and his mother to get to the checkout.

"You'll never guess what Jamie came to buy," his mother said before he got there.

From the look on his face, Jamie could tell that what she came to buy didn't even come close to making his list of things he wanted to know.

"Didn't you want to get to the grocery store, Mom?" He checked his watch again, reminding Jamie of his clockwatching at their meeting last week. Either Eli really wanted to see his football game or he had a compulsion about time.

"She needs one of those valve things you came for. Why don't you show her where they are?"

Eli lifted his gaze to the overhead fluorescent lights, and Jamie took pity on him. "No need. I see the plumbing sign over aisle eight. I'll go look. I brought the old one." She lifted up the valve in her hand. "If I can't find one that matches, I'll ask. That's what the associates are here for."

"No, my grocery shopping can wait a few minutes. JR doesn't mind, do you?"

Obviously, Leah had missed Eli's mumbled, "But the kickoff won't wait." Or she'd ignored it.

"Not at all." A muscle worked in his jaw.

Jamie followed him to aisle eight. "You can ditch me here. I'll ask for help if I need it." She perused the display. "But I don't. This looks like the right one." She tapped the package with her fingernail.

He reached over and lifted it from the hook. "Let me see your old one."

Jamie handed it over, although she was sure it was the right one.

"It is. See the model number matches."

"Uh-huh."

He tilted his head and looked at her for a moment. Did he really think matching model numbers would be an all-new concept to her? She'd figured that out years ago when John was on his first deployment and the water hose on her washing machine had sprung a leak.

She took the valve back. "Let's check out. Maybe you can still catch most of your game."

He cracked a smile and her knees went weak. When he wasn't being austere and all business, Eli was attractive in that man's man way that many women found appealing. Okay. She was one of those many women.

"Only if we don't run into too many people she knows at the grocery store that she has to 'just' say hi to."

"She does like to visit."

"With everyone."

Jamie laughed. "True. Tell you what." She succumbed to the lighter, more jovial side of Eli she was seeing for the first time. "Why don't I take her over to the supercenter? I have a few things I could pick up, and we haven't seen each other in a while. It's no problem. Her house is on the way home."

"What about your kids?" His expression hardened.

"What about them?" She didn't need another lecture from Eli Payton, Super Guidance Counselor, about spending time or not spending time with her kids. She'd much preferred the Eli-Payton-shopping-with-his-mother version of the man.

"If you have to know, which you don't, the girls are selling Girl Scout cookies with their Brownie and Girl Scout troops at the Grand Union, and I dropped Myles off to snowblow the driveway for one of the midwives I work with here in Ticonderoga. No chance of him escaping before I pick him up."

Eli glared at her. She probably should have skipped the sarcasm, but he'd provoked her. Where did he get off thinking he was in charge of her and her family in any way, shape or manner?

He shook his head almost imperceptibly. "I didn't mean to sound like I was criticizing you."

"But you did. It's one of my hot spots. People comment about single parents. Ask your friend Neal. It's not like I chose to be a single mother."

Uncertainty flickered in his steel-gray eyes, tempering her irritation. He looked genuinely contrite.

"We should check out." He started up the aisle.

Jamie caught up with him. "It's okay. Your afternoon doesn't seem to be going as you'd planned." She knew he'd asked about the kids out of genuine concern and was willing to let go of her defensiveness. Oddly, it seemed important to her all of a sudden that Eli see her as someone other than a mother, even though that's what she was. The mother of one of his students.

"You've got that right. You don't mind taking Mom shopping? I really appreciate it."

"Not at all. All I have planned is to install this." She held up the new valve.

"By yourself?" He glanced at her and halted his step. "Wrong thing to say—again."

She nodded. "Wrong thing to say. I do a lot of home maintenance. My aunt and uncle gave my husband and me a great home repair book as a wedding present. Neither one of us knew anything. Turned out I was a lot better at it than he was." A qualm rippled through her at having criticized John. But she hadn't really. She *was* better and over the years had collected a fair amount of experience. Moreover, she enjoyed it.

"Good for you. I haven't had much experience with handy female civilians. But I've known a lot of very resourceful military wives."

Jamie wanted to shout at him that she wasn't military, hadn't been military, didn't want to be associated with the military. She had been, though. And had chosen that life path with John, fully aware of her choice—as fully aware as an eighteen-year-old could be.

But Eli didn't need to know that. And if he were like any of the soldiers she'd known, wouldn't want to hear it.

"I do what I have to do. Myles is a big help, too, when I run into something that's a two-person job."

"That's a productive use of his time."

Jamie's temper sparked and ebbed. What was it about Eli that made her think everything he said was a comment on her parenting skills? Maybe it was the nature of his job, although Myles's former guidance counselor, Erin Ryder, hadn't had the same effect on her. She glanced at Eli's profile and her heart did a traitorous flip-flop that wiped away her annoyance with him. Eli had several effects on her that Erin hadn't.

"Did you find what you needed?" Leah's voice pulled Jamie from her thoughts. She felt a blush tinge her cheeks.

"Yes." Jamie motioned Eli to check out ahead of her.

His mother frowned when he placed his purchase on the checkout stand.

"Eli said you need to go to the supercenter. I can take you. I need to pick up a few things, too." Jamie lowered her voice. "I think he wants to watch that football game Harry was talking about."

Out of the corner of her eye, Jamie caught Eli giving her a thumbs-up. She started at the boyish gesture. It seemed out of character for Eli, or at least for the picture she'd formed of him.

"Oh." Bewilderment laced Leah's voice. "I didn't catch that. I was going to suggest Eli go over to your house after we got back and install that part for you."

"No need. Myles and I can handle it."

Disappointment clouded Leah's face.

Eli coughed, and Jamie stifled a laugh. Leah was

matchmaking, and he must have found it as preposterous as Jamie did.

"You have the kids and your job. You shouldn't have to do house repairs, too. I'll send Eli over some evening next week to do it for you."

This time Eli's cough came out more as the choke he was trying to cover.

Leah waved him off. "Go ahead and watch your game. I'll shop with Jamie. We can get in some girl talk."

Jamie had a feeling Leah's girl talk might evolve into boy talk. One "boy" in particular. Maybe while they were on the topic, she could convince Leah that she didn't need Eli to help her with her plumbing. Or maybe Leah's current art project would absorb her attention to the exclusion of everything else, as often happened, and she'd forget all about her offer.

The last thing Jamie needed was more quality time with Eli. He couldn't seem to open his mouth without saying something that rubbed her the wrong way. Of course, if he stopped talking and just stood around looking good, she might get used to him.

Eli found his friend Drew Stacey's truck in the driveway as he pulled up to the small winterized cottage he was renting on Paradox Lake. He parked next to the truck and got out.

"Hey, I thought you'd stood me up," Drew said.

Eli's mind went blank for a moment. *The game.*

He'd invited Drew over to watch the game. He was becoming as absentminded as his mother. Between repairing his mother's heating system and the distraction of running into Jamie at the hardware store, he'd forgotten about Drew. Maybe he should cut Mom some slack. Civilian life was proving less predictable than his former life.

"Time got away from me."

"Now, that's a first," Drew said.

Eli rubbed the back of his neck. "I had to go into Ticonderoga and get a release valve for Mom's heating system. She wanted to come along to pick up some groceries."

"Let me guess. She ran into someone she knew."

Drew obviously knew his mother. "Several someones." Eli opened the door and the men went in the house. "Including Jamie Glasser." Eli winced. He had no idea why he'd added that.

"Better watch out," Drew said, making himself comfortable on Eli's couch.

Eli picked up the remote and flicked the TV on. The screen flashed a zero-zero score and went to a commercial break. "How's that?"

"After Jamie's husband was killed, your mother helped her out. All of us at church did. But your mother more than many. She said she could relate to Jamie's situation having been a young widow herself. And having a son in the military."

"That sounds like Mom. She has a big heart."

"That she does. And it was broken when Jamie and the kids stopped coming to church and she couldn't convince her to return."

"Jamie was a member of Community Church?"

"Yeah, she was one of the charter members of our Singles Plus group, sang in the choir and often helped with the women's group fund-raisers."

"And she just stopped coming?"

"Pretty much."

Eli would have thought that, if her faith had been as strong as her church activities seemed to indicate, she would have drawn on that faith. That's what he'd always done.

"Jamie's bitter. John was supposed to have come home in less than a month. Pastor Joel, your mother—no one's been able to break through that bitterness."

"Tough situation." One he'd seen too often. And one he didn't need to get involved in. "I'm going to get a drink. Do you want anything?" Eli needed to distance himself from Drew's words and the pain they recalled.

"I'll take a cola if you have one."

"Sure thing."

Eli walked into the kitchen and opened the refrigerator. He'd been stunned when he'd learned that his ex-fiancée had been killed. And he'd lost other friends. So he knew a little of what Jamie had gone through. He knew the bitterness, too. The questions about how a loving God could allow the atrocities of war. But he'd found solace in prayer. Turned to, not away from Him.

He grabbed two sodas and closed the refrigerator with his elbow. Who was he to judge Jamie's actions? Still he pitied her for not taking the healing love offered her. And he pitied her kids more for Jamie's denying them that healing power by taking them away from church.

"What did I miss?" he asked as he returned to the living room and tossed Drew his cola.

"Incomplete pass." Drew waited a second and popped the tab on the can.

Eli settled in the worn recliner. Thoughts of Jamie and his mother clouded his concentration on the game. Army called for a timeout and the station went to another commercial.

"You know you never told me what I needed to watch out for," Eli mused.

"Huh?"

"When I'd said we'd run into Jamie, you said I'd better watch out."

"Oh, that. Your mother has become something of a matchmaker."

Eli groaned, leaning his head back and closing his eyes. An image of Jamie's face lighting up with an impish smile when he'd given her his thumbs-up signal in the hardware store flashed in his head. "Jamie and me? No way. She's not my type." So why couldn't he get the woman out of his thoughts?

Chapter Four

"Eli Payton."

The woman's voice filtering back from the reception area jerked Jamie's attention from the patient chart she was updating on her iPad. Eli was here? At the birthing center? She looked through the window separating the nursing station from reception.

"Has agreed to cover my classes for me," Becca Norton finished. "So any time of the day is okay for my appointment."

"The new guidance counselor? My daughter loves him. And he's not bad on the eyes, either," the office assistant said.

"I can't argue with that and neither would my junior girls. Some of them find the need to visit the guidance office daily to discuss their college and career goals."

Jamie's stomach clenched and she tapped the tablet's screen too sharply. Seriously, she couldn't be jealous of a bunch of starry-eyed sixteen-year-olds. Nor should she be jealous of Becca. Jamie was hard-pressed to think of anyone who suited her less than Eli Payton did. If, that is, she was looking for some-one to suit, which she wasn't. She had more than enough in her life with work and the kids.

As for Eli and Becca, Jamie's rational side said they might be good together. They were both edu-cators and active in the Hazardtown Community Church. He'd offered to cover Becca's classes for her doctor's appointments. There could already be some interest there. Jamie tamped down the less positive feelings her emotional side had set loose.

She should drop some hints about Becca to Leah the next time she ran into her, so Leah could chan-nel her matchmaking efforts elsewhere. A good part of her shopping trip with the older woman had con-sisted of Leah touting Eli's virtues and how much he liked kids. How he realized that, at his age, he needed to be open to the possibility of the "right" woman already having children. Leah had assured Jamie that he was.

Her cell phone buzzed in her pocket, halting Ja-mie's thoughts and the empty hole that had started to blossom in her stomach when she'd pictured Eli and Becca together. It was most likely one of the kids. She frowned. They knew they weren't sup-posed to call her during office hours unless it was an emergency.

"Hello," she answered without checking the caller ID.

"Hi, Jamie. It's Emily. You busy?"

Jamie regretted the irritation in her greeting. "I'm at work, but I've finished my last appointment. What's up?"

"I need a favor. Drew is taking the youth group sledding at the golf course tomorrow. Maybe Myles told you about it. The kids planned it at the last meeting."

Jamie tensed. Was she going to ask her to allow Myles to go? Eli had probably told Drew about her blowup with him after he'd driven Myles home from the meeting and Drew had asked his wife to clear the sledding with Jamie beforehand. She was torn. She wanted Myles to be involved in good activities. But she didn't want him to be taught to depend on faith to get through life. John's death had shown her the futility of that.

She shook off the tension. More likely she was making something out of nothing. Guys were more closemouthed about things. Emily was probably calling about something else altogether, like borrowing her kids' sleds.

"No, Myles didn't mention it." But, then, he hadn't said much of anything to her in the past couple of weeks, except when Jamie had asked him a direct question.

"I thought he might be coming since he was at the meeting. He took a permission slip."

"Oh."

"No matter. Could you come and chaperone? It's tomorrow from one to four. I know. Short notice. I'm supposed to be the girls' chaperone, but both of my kids had some kind of bug the past few days, and now I'm way behind on a deadline. I need to work tomorrow."

Three hours of chaperoning the youth group outing meant three hours with Eli—probably, the more congenial jeans-and-Henley-shirt Eli she'd glimpsed at the hardware store. Her pulse quickened. No, it wasn't a good idea. Even if Myles went, Jamie still had the girls and was on call.

Emily filled the growing silence. "Rose and Opal can come, too. It's strictly a social event. I understand you've distanced yourself from church, and I respect that."

Church wasn't all she'd distanced herself from, but she didn't need to get into that with Emily or anyone else. "I don't know. I'm on call with Kelly tomorrow." Even though it was a reasonable excuse, it wasn't good enough to stop the twinge of guilt that pricked her. Emily *had* taken the girls after school the day she'd been delayed by her meeting with Eli, even though Emily had been busy working.

"I'm sure you could leave if you got a call. I've asked everyone I can think of. No one's available."

There was a time when Jamie would have been the first person Emily would have called, not the last. Or wouldn't have had to call at all because Jamie would have already volunteered to chaperone. A yearning to belong to something beyond work and family pulled at her. It was time for her to get involved in activities again. They didn't have to be connected to church. She could volunteer with Rose and Opal's Girl Scout troops or at school. If Myles ran track in the spring as Eli had suggested, she could join the sports boosters. They were always looking for help.

"Are you still there?" Emily asked.

"Yes." She had to stop the woolgathering and simply tell her friend no.

"Good. With the spotty cell coverage around here, I thought I'd lost you. Drew and I would really appreciate it if you can cover for me. He doesn't want to have to cancel and disappoint the kids." Emily paused. "If it makes any difference, Eli won't be there."

Jamie cringed inside. Emily did know about the friction between her and Eli. For all Jamie knew, everyone did. Everyone but his mother.

"Sure, why not?" She relented. What could it hurt?

Saturday turned out to be one of those perfect winter days, the sky so blue it almost hurt her eyes and the temperature low enough to make the snow crisp and ideal for sledding without being bitterly cold.

"Put a move on it, girls. Get your saucers out of the garage. We're supposed to be at the golf course in fifteen minutes."

Although the group was gathering at the church for carpooling, Jamie had told Drew she would meet them at the Schroon Lake Country Club golf course.

"Mom, do we need the padding for the toboggan?" Myles called from the garage. "I can't find it."

Considering the searching abilities of most teenage boys, that wasn't saying much. She started toward the garage.

"Never mind. I found it." A moment later, he appeared at the garage door with the padded toboggan in tow. They loaded it into the car, and Myles lifted the girls' saucers in.

Everyone piled in, the girls vibrating with excitement at being included in an event with the big kids. Under his usual gruff, noncommittal attitude, Myles seemed to be happy, too. Jamie snuck a look at his relaxed profile as she drove State Route 74 to Schroon Lake. Since she'd told him about her filling in for Emily today, she'd had her old Myles back. The joy of having her goofy, lovable lug of a teen boy around lightened Jamie's heart.

As usual, Jamie and her crew arrived at the country club first. She couldn't help it. She was perpetually early, which was one reason Eli's attention to her arrival and the clock had aggravated her so during their first meeting. If she'd known about the meeting she would have been on time or let him know she wouldn't be. But no need to ruin her good mood by dredging up something that happened in the past and couldn't be changed.

"Let's unload our stuff. I'm sure everyone else will be here in a minute." She checked her watch. *Or ten.*

"I knew you'd be here," Drew said when he pulled up and got out of his pickup.

"You know me. When I first started driving, my dad drilled into me to always leave with enough time to change a tire if I had a flat and still be on time."

"How's that worked?"

"Can't really tell you, since I've never had a flat tire. Of course, I'm never late, either." *Or almost never late.*

Drew laughed. "Emily and I really appreciate your helping out."

"Glad to." She hadn't realized how much until just now.

The other drivers started arriving, and the kids spilled out into the parking lot with an assortment of sleds.

"Ready, girls?" Drew asked, motioning Rose and Opal to follow him. Myles had already sauntered over to Tanner's mother's car.

"And no big deal if Kelly calls you in for a birth," Drew called over his shoulder. "Eli changed his plans. He said he could cut out of his American Legion meeting in time to get here by two at the latest."

Jamie stared at their retreating backs. It surprised her that Eli would skirt a Legion commitment but not that he still had a hand in the military. John had planned to join the U.S. Army Reserve when he mustered out of the army. Once in the service, always in the service. She'd learned that as a young military wife. The service always came first.

Jamie pocketed her keys and trudged across the snow-covered parking lot to catch up with the others. Had Drew told Eli she was filling in for Emily? Was that why he'd changed his mind about being able to help? Her traitorous heart skipped a beat. If so, it had to be because he didn't trust her to watch the kids, not because of any desire to see her. His attitude at their meeting had said to her that he thought she was an inept mother who couldn't take care of her own child. Why would he think she'd be any better with other people's children? Not that it mattered, beyond the fact that his critical attitude aggravated her. She didn't need to prove anything to him. For all she knew, he treated all parents the same as he treated her. Jamie breathed in the clear cold winter air and released it. But, for whatever reason, his treatment of her did matter.

* * *

Eli shielded the sun from his eyes and surveyed the figures at the top of the golf course hill. He spotted Jamie's purple jacket right off. At least he thought it was hers. It was the same color as the coat she'd worn to their last meeting. The figure turned. Black curls peeked out from the sides and front of her multihued ski hat. A sense of satisfaction filled him. He knew it was her. He climbed the hill, surprised at how much he'd warmed at the minor exertion. He hadn't thought he'd let himself get that much out of fighting shape.

As he reached the top, two smaller kids grabbed Jamie's gloved hands and pulled her toward a toboggan. Evidently, along with the youth group teens, Jamie had Myles's younger sisters to contend with, too. Good thing he hadn't had any difficulty leaving the meeting. The guys had already worked out all of the details for the teen rifle course, and he hadn't really been needed. Not as much as he was needed here.

"Hey, man." Drew lifted a hand in greeting.

Eli joined him.

"The kids wanted to have toboggan races. I've had Jamie here setting up the heats and I've been clocking the finishes at the bottom. We're taking a break so she can make a run with Rose and Opal. She's okay with them using their saucers on the smaller run but didn't want them taking the toboggan down alone."

Eli nodded his agreement with her decision. "How many kids came?"

"About twenty. All the regulars and a few guests, older kids' boyfriends and girlfriends. Lends a new dimension to the chaperoning." Drew moved his head to the left to a lone couple snuggled close, waiting for the last round of racers to return with the toboggans.

"I can think of a whole lot of worse places for them to be getting close than sledding with the youth group. Why don't I walk over and say hi?"

"You do that," Drew said. "And I'll go back to my station downhill."

Drew was going to leave him here with Jamie? Well, here with her when she got back up from her run with her daughters. After a second of ridiculous and unfounded apprehension, reality clicked in. Of course. She'd need more help up here shepherding the teens and keeping an eye on her girls than Drew would at the bottom of the run. He whistled as he walked over to the young couple Drew had pointed out.

"Hey, Seth."

"Hi, Mr. Payton."

While most of the youth group members called Drew by his first name, Eli had stuck with the more formal address, since he was most of the members' guidance counselor at school.

The boy loosened his vice grip on the girl's waist and she lifted her head from his shoulder. "This is my girlfriend, Ava. She's from Ticonderoga. I might have mentioned her when I was talking to you about college and stuff."

Ava tipped her head toward Seth and her eyes narrowed.

Eli tamped down a grin. Looked like Seth was in trouble.

"He's cool. I was sounding him out about our plans."

The girl still looked skeptical. "Nice to meet you."

"You, too. Are you having a good time?"

"Yeah." She shrugged.

Eli remembered Seth's plans. Drew was on the right track keeping an eye on them. The couple planned to move to Albany in the fall, where she had a scholarship to St. Rose College. Seth was going to work and attend the state university there part-time. Seth hadn't come right out and said it, but Eli had a strong impression that Ava wasn't going to be living in the campus dorms.

Ah, to be young and in love.

Too bad it rarely lasted. He hadn't been much older than Seth when he'd been engaged. His former fiancée had had a couple of years on him. She'd been almost twenty-one.

A splat of snow on the back of his leg, followed by a high-pitched giggle, drew him from the couple and his musings.

"Opal!"

He turned as Jamie crested the hill. The cold had put a rosy blush on her cheeks and the sunlight kissed her flawless skin. She looked barely older than Ava did. But Myles had to be fourteen or fifteen. She must be close to his own age, thirty-eight. Unless she and her husband had been one of those young loves that had lasted. A sharp pang of jealousy pricked him, followed by disgust that he was jealous of a fallen comrade.

Jamie's breath caught when Eli turned, even though she knew it was him. He was taller and had broader shoulders than any of the teens, and his posture shouted "in command."

"Apologize to Mr. Payton for throwing snow at him."

"You mean him?" Opal pointed at Eli. "I didn't throw my snowball at him. I threw it at Rose and missed."

"Opal!" Jamie gritted her teeth to keep the screech out of her voice. Eli didn't need to think all of her kids were incorrigible.

"Okay, okay." Opal trudged over and planted herself toe-to-toe with Eli. She tilted her head back and looked him in the eye. "Sorry my snowball missed my sister and hit you."

Jamie clenched her fists. The little girl's tone clearly said she was sorrier she'd missed Rose than hit Eli.

A smile tugged at the corner of his mouth and his eyes twinkled. "Apology accepted."

Jamie unfolded her fingers.

"Hey, you're pretty big," Opal said. "I bet you weigh a lot."

Jamie lifted her gaze to the cloudless sky.

A deep full laugh rumbled from Eli's chest and stopped Jamie's reprimand before she could vocalize it.

"I mean," Opal said, "you could make the toboggan go really fast. I thought Mommy could 'cause she's gotten so fat her favorite jeans don't fit. But we didn't go that fast."

"Is that right?" Eli gave Jamie a once-over, his smile broadening.

She looked around to see if there was a snow pile nearby that she could bury herself in.

"Yeah, it was fun, but I would have liked to go faster."

"Opal, that's enough. Drew is signaling me to get the next heat of races going." Well, he *was* motioning someone about something.

"Mommy! But I have a good idea I want to tell Mr….Mr…."

"Payton," Eli filled in, obviously enjoying himself from the look on his face.

"Mr. Payton. I'm Opal Susan Glasser."

"Nice to meet you, Opal Susan Glasser."

Jamie sensed rather than saw the youth group members congregating behind her.

"You can just call me Opal." She turned to Jamie, dancing from one foot to the other. "Mommy, can I tell him my good idea?"

"Go ahead." At least she still had a modicum of authority.

"If you and Mommy and me rode the toboggan, we could really fly."

"What about me?" Rose sidled up next to Jamie.

Opal bit her lip. "I guess. You'd add some extra weight. What do you think, Mr. Payton?"

"I agree. I think your sister would add some extra weight."

"No!" Opal stomped her foot in the snow and laughed. "I mean about us racing."

Eli's gaze caught Jamie's. The winter sun glinted off his steel-blue eyes, or was it a sparkle of humor? Jamie warmed. He was good with kids. But that was his job, wasn't it?

"We just went," Jamie said. "We'll have to wait our turn again."

"But Mr. Payton didn't. He hasn't had a turn. We

could show him how to do it." Opal reached for the rope to the toboggan.

Jamie pulled it back out of her reach. She wasn't nearly as anxious as Opal to pile on the toboggan with Eli. She ran her gaze from his snow-crusted boots up his long legs to the navy blue ski cap covering his sandy brown hair. By himself, he'd take up most of the length of the sled.

"I'll tell you what," Eli said. "We'll run the rest of the heats until we have a winner. Then, you and your sister…"

"Rose," her older daughter filled in.

"And your mom can challenge the winner."

Opal surveyed the teens gathered around them. "Good deal. We'll win for sure."

"Don't count on it, squirt." Myles walked up behind Opal and tugged her braid. He glanced from Jamie to Eli. A guarded look replaced his teasing grin.

"Hey," Drew shouted from below. "What's going on up there? Let's get these races going."

Jamie handed Myles the toboggan. "Okay, who's up?"

The nine teens who had won their heats lined up a few feet behind the crest of the hill with two on the toboggans and the third member of each team standing to the side ready to push them off to a running start.

"Do you want to do the honors?" Jamie pulled a green bandana from her coat pocket and held it out to Eli. "The green flag. We're improvising."

"Ah, you've got this all organized."

He pulled the bandana from her hand and gave her a lopsided grin that allowed her to ignore the surprise she'd detected in his voice.

"Is everyone ready?" she asked.

"Ready. Yes. Yo." The teams each answered.

Eli raised the bandana. "On your mark. Get set." He dropped the cloth. "Go."

Opal and Rose jumped up and down. "Go, Myles! Go, Tanner!"

Drew raised his hands over his head as Myles's toboggan flew by him first. He jumped off the toboggan and threw his hands in the air with a "whoop." They ran another heat with Myles's team coming in first again. It lifted Jamie's spirits to see him having fun and enjoying himself.

"Come on, Mr. Payton." Opal grabbed Eli's hand as the teens returned to the top of the hill. "We have to beat Myles and Tanner."

Jamie visualized them all crowded onto the toboggan, which seemed to have shrunk since she'd unloaded it in the parking lot. "You don't have to do this."

"Sure I do. I gave my word."

Of course, he had. Jamie eyed the toboggan. She

could sit in the front to steer and the girls could sit behind her as a buffer, with Eli in the back.

"Can I sit in front?" Rose asked.

"No, I want to," Opal said. "She sat in front last time."

"That sounds good to me," Eli said. "You, Rose, your mom and me. How does that sound to you, Mom?"

Jamie searched her brain for a good reason to say no. "I don't think so. Opal's not big enough to steer the toboggan."

Opal put her hands on her hips and opened her mouth.

"Agreed," Eli said.

"But, you said." The little girl sputtered.

"I did. You and Rose can sit up front and your mom can steer from behind you."

The satisfied expression on Eli's face said that he thought he had it all solved. Except his solution had her sandwiched between the girls and him.

"Hey, are you guys going to race or not?" Tanner shouted. Myles and their other teammate were already in place ready to go.

Both girls looked at her expectantly. "Come on, Mom," Rose said. "It's all right with me if Opal sits in front."

"Okay, then." Jamie relented. She was being silly. It was only a couple-minute ride.

Jamie lined their toboggan up parallel to Myles

and Tanner's and held it while the girls climbed on. She followed, leaving Eli as much room behind her as she could. He stood to the right, his hands resting on her shoulders. She craned her head around to signal they were ready and, when her gaze caught his, a spark of energy shot through her. The girls' enthusiasm must be catching.

"Where's the flag?" Seth called out.

"I've got it," Eli said. He raised his hands from her shoulders to pull the bandana out of his back pocket where he'd stuffed it after the last heat.

She shivered as the light pressure lifted and wiggled a little closer to Rose.

"Mom, you're squishing me."

"Sorry. I wanted to make sure Mr. Payton had enough room."

Rose peered around her mother. "He's not that big."

Jamie gripped the rope and stayed where she was.

"Here you are." Eli handed the bandana to Seth and returned to them.

Jamie braced herself for him to put his hands back on her shoulders.

"All set?"

"Yes," she answered without looking at him. Rose and Opal echoed her agreement.

"Then, let's race."

At Seth's "Go!" Eli pushed them three long strides and scrambled on behind Jamie. As he wrapped his arms around her waist, she determined that, contrary to Rose's assertion, she hadn't given him an inch too much space.

Halfway down the hill, with their toboggan in the lead, a dog darted up the hill into Myles's path.

"Watch out," she and Eli shouted in unison.

Myles yanked the control ropes hard to avoid the dog and sent his toboggan in a trajectory straight for the front of theirs.

Fear paralyzed Jamie for a moment and a second too late, she pulled the left-side rope as hard as she could to steer them out of Myles's way, but it wasn't enough and the rope broke. Myles and Tanner were headed directly for Opal.

Chapter Five

Eli felt every muscle in Jamie's body stiffen when she saw the boys' toboggan careening toward them.

"The rope broke," she screamed.

"Rose, grab Opal," he ordered as he stretched his right leg and rolled all four of them off into the snow. The other toboggan smashed into theirs and continued down the hill.

Eli jumped to his feet. "Are you all right?" He offered Jamie a hand up.

She grasped it tightly, rose and shook off the snow. "I'm fine."

Her words released the tension dammed up inside him. He stepped over and helped Rose and Opal up.

"Why did you do that?" Opal glared at him. "We were winning."

"Opal, that's no way to talk to Mr. Payton. He kept us from getting hurt."

"I don't care. He's not our boss. He's not Daddy."

Eli didn't know where that came from and, by the stony look on Jamie's face, neither did she. All he'd done was keep them safe. He jerked his head away and looked up at the descending yellow-orange sun. What was with him? He was questioning his trained instincts because of a child's accusation.

"Stop right there, young lady."

He turned to see Opal stomping down the hill. Jamie started after her.

"Mom. Mommy." The quiver in Rose's voice and her use of Mommy drew both his and Jamie's attention. The girl had sat back down in the snow. "My leg hurts like it did last summer at camp when my kneecap slid out of place."

Jamie looked from Rose to Opal, who was now most of the way down the hill.

"I'll go after her," Eli said.

Relief flooded Jamie's face. "Thanks."

He looked over at Rose. A tear streaked one cheek.

"If it's her kneecap, I should be able to snap it back in place. I've done it before. We'll be fine," Jamie reassured him.

He jogged down the hill after Opal. Jamie's firm, calm handling of the situation—make that situations—with the girls impressed him. If it was an example of typical day-to-day life with kids, parenting was a lot like combat.

Eli reached Opal at the same time Myles did. Her

brother must have seen her stomping downhill when he and Tanner were headed back up.

Myles reached for his sister, and she kicked him in the shin. "Don't touch me."

Myles rubbed his leg. "You are going to be in such trouble with Mom."

"I don't care. We were ahead and then you cheated and ruined everything." Opal burst into tears.

"Go ahead." Eli motioned Myles uphill. "Opal and I will head over to the clubhouse. I hear they have hot chocolate there."

"She kicks me, and you take *her* for hot chocolate." Myles looked up the hill at his mother and shook his head.

"Go help your mother with Rose. I'll handle this."

"Whatever."

Opal looked at her brother.

"Yeah, you can go have hot chocolate with him." The teen yanked his toboggan and stomped away much like his sister had earlier.

Eli took Opal's hand. "You weren't nice to your brother."

Opal shrugged her shoulders and sniffled.

"The race was supposed to be for fun. It didn't matter who won." Eli opened the clubhouse door and followed the little girl in.

"Yes, it did."

"Sit here." He pulled out a chair for her in the

small snack area. "I'll get the hot chocolate and we can talk."

Her coffee-brown eyes, so like her brother's and mother's, flashed defiance, but she nodded.

Eli got their drinks and returned to the table. He handed Opal a cup.

"Thanks." She kept her eyes focused on the cup.

He slid into the seat across from her, unzipping his jacket but leaving it on since the clubhouse wasn't a lot warmer than outside. "So tell me why it was so important for you to win the race." He sipped his hot chocolate as he waited for her answer.

"Not me, us. It was important for us to win so Mommy would be impressed with you. You would have made us win. That would have impressed her. We were going a lot faster with you on the toboggan than Mommy and Rose and I did when we went down before."

He was certain winning would not make any difference in Jamie's opinion of him, and he wasn't sure he wanted to know why Opal wanted him to impress her mother.

"There's this father-daughter dance at school. They have it every year." Her words poured out. "Daddy was home one year and went with Rose. But I wasn't in school yet, so I couldn't go. Mommy said she'd go with us, but that's weird. It's not the mother-daughter dance."

Eli could see where this might be going, but he had to ask. "What does that have to do with me?"

Opal sighed, as if he should already know the answer, which he was afraid he did. "When Emily watched us after school that day Mommy and Myles were meeting with you, I heard her tell Drew that Mommy should start going out again. That it's been almost two years since Daddy didn't come home and Mommy needed fun with grown-up friends."

Opal's words kicked him in the gut. He wondered how often she'd seen her father. Had she known him at all? She talked about his death as if it were only a matter of him not coming home when he was scheduled to. Like he might return later. Had John Glasser had regrets about how much he was missing out on being away for so much of his kids' lives? Eli studied the black curls that had escaped Opal's braid and framed her face, just like her mother's curls. Glasser would have had to be a fool if he hadn't. He revised his hasty assessment of the man. Jamie struck Eli as a woman who wouldn't suffer a fool.

"If Mommy liked you, you could be her boyfriend and take her out and make her happy, like Emily said. And if you were her boyfriend, you could take me and Rose to the dance. Amy Bryant's mother's boyfriend is taking her."

The hope in her wide eyes got to him. "Opal," he said as gently as he could, "I can't be your mother's boyfriend simply because you want me to be."

"But if she liked you, you could be." A single tear slid down her cheek.

"Honey, that's not—"

"No!" She pushed away from the table, sloshing hot chocolate on its surface. "Leave me alone. I'm going to the girls' room." She ran toward the lavatory.

Eli rose to follow her.

"Let her go," said the woman who had sold him the hot chocolates. "If she's not out in a minute, I'll go in and check on her. The back door is locked. The only place she can come is back here."

The woman had looked familiar. Now he recognized her from church.

"I'm Karen Hill. My husband and son own Hill's Auto Repair. I think you may have gone to school with my youngest brother, Mark."

"We played football together. How's he doing? I haven't run into him since I returned."

"You wouldn't have. He lives out near Seattle, has a company that designs computer games and apps. Stuff like that."

"I can see that. He was a wiz at math. And Ninja Gaiden."

Eli glanced over toward the hall to the restrooms. Shouldn't Opal be back by now?

"Sad, isn't it?" Karen asked. "Those poor kids without a father. And Jamie, so young to be widowed. Can you imagine?"

"Yeah, it's tough."

Karen raised her hand and covered her mouth. "Sorry. I'd forgotten about your father. You do know what they're going through."

Eli shifted in the chair. "Uh, would you mind checking on Opal?"

"Sure. We'll be right back." Karen hustled across the room.

He finished off his hot chocolate in one swig and made a face. The drink had gone cold and bitter. When Karen didn't return immediately, he stood and walked to the hall. The air temperature dropped as he turned the corner and saw Karen pushing open the glass door at the end of the hallway. The door she'd said was locked.

She looked back over her shoulder. "Opal wasn't in the ladies' room." Concern laced her words. "This door is supposed to be locked."

"There's no place else in the building she could have gone without our seeing her?" he demanded.

She shook her head. "I checked the storage closet to see if she was hiding in there. She wasn't. The only other room this hall connects to is the one we were in."

Eli stepped in front of her and pushed the door open wider.

"I called Jerry, our maintenance guy, to look for her. He's out on the snowmobile."

He stared out at the expanse of snow-covered terrain. His chest tightened. He'd lost Jamie's daughter. "Thanks. I'll go try to follow her footprints. It shouldn't take me long to catch up with her." He checked his watch. How long had she been gone? Had she even used the bathroom or gone right out when she'd left him?

Her footprints tracked through the snow, meandering around a small pond before mixing with a hundred others—some heading up the hill, some going toward the parking lot and the road.

Eli closed his eyes. *Please, Lord, keep Opal safe.* He looked up the hill and didn't see Jamie's jacket among the figures congregating at the top. But he did see Drew, who waved him up.

When he reached Drew, Eli's heart was pounding—much more from fear about Opal than the exertion of sprinting up the hill. "Where's Jamie?"

Drew looked at him sideways. "She had to take Rose to urgent care."

The pounding picked up tempo. "Oh, man. I've lost Opal." Eli glanced from side to side to make sure none of the teens had overheard him.

Drew burst out laughing.

"What's so funny?" Eli's fingers itched to wipe the grin off his friend's face. Hadn't Drew gotten what he'd said? "Opal got mad at me at the clubhouse and took off. I can't find her."

Drew caught his breath. "She's fine. She's with Jamie. Sara saw her outside the clubhouse and walked her back. Opal does stuff like that all of the time. It drives Jamie crazy."

Drew was driving him crazy. "It didn't occur to you to send someone down to tell me that?"

"No, I thought you'd asked Sara to bring her back. Opal said something about you talking with a lady at the snack bar." Drew arched an eyebrow. "Didn't want to interrupt anything."

"Right, Karen Hill. Was Jamie mad?"

"About what?"

Drew had to be kidding. "My not bringing Opal back. I'm not Jamie's favorite person as it is."

Drew's eyes narrowed and one corner of his mouth tilted up. "But you'd like to be. Go for it. She didn't seem mad at all to me. As I said, Opal's done that before."

His friend's ribbing rubbed him the wrong way. But he was too drained to answer the challenge. "It must be about time to go. I'll start rounding up the kids." As he walked away, his earlier thought echoed in his head. *Jamie wasn't a woman who would suffer a fool.*

"Mommy," Opal said as Jamie drove the girls home from the urgent care center. "I'm glad Rose's knee is okay."

"That's nice of you to be concerned about your sister."

"Yeah, you know the father-daughter dance at school is next week."

Jamie's chest tightened. She didn't know why Opal was so focused on the event. The elementary grades had the dinner-dance every year. Originally, it had been called the father-daughter dinner-dance, and that name had stuck even though the school hadn't called it that in years. Officially, it was the Winter Dinner-Dance. The idea was to get dads more involved, but escorts weren't limited to fathers. Brothers, uncles, grandfathers, friends and even mothers were welcome.

"I don't think you'll have to take us."

"Is that right?" Opal must have asked Drew to take them. Jamie would be sure to tell him he didn't have to, as he had enough to do with his own family.

"Yes. Mr. Payton is going to take us."

Jamie swallowed wrong and choked. "What?" she coughed out.

"I asked him when he bought me hot chocolate."

"Sweetie, why?"

"It's lame to go to a daddy dance with your mother, and Mr. Payton seems like he'd be a good daddy."

Jamie blinked back tears. Opal seemed to have accepted John's death the easiest of the three kids, probably because she'd seen him so rarely. He'd been deployed to the Middle East most of her short life. She glanced at her daughters in the rearview mirror. Or had she been so wrapped up in Myles acting out that she'd missed her daughters' needs?

She swallowed and tried to imagine Eli's reaction to Opal's request and how it may have affected Opal. A snapshot of his lopsided grin when he'd pulled the green bandana from her hand to start the toboggan race imbedded itself in her brain. She loosened her grip on the steering wheel. Opal's assessment of Eli might be right. He was good with kids. She shook his picture from her mind. Thinking of Eli as daddy material was a dangerous direction she needed to steer Opal, and herself, clear of.

"What exactly did you say to Mr. Payton?"

"I told him that if you liked him… You do like him, don't you?"

"Yes, I like him." She did like him, even if they had their differences.

"I said if you liked him, he could be your boyfriend, and he could take me and Rose to the dance."

No wonder Eli sent Opal back up the hill with Sara. He probably needed to recover from that bomb.

"You are such a baby to tell him that," Rose said.

"Am not."

"Rose, no name-calling."

"But, Mom. Can you imagine what he thought?"

Jamie could imagine, and that was a problem.

"Let your sister finish."

Rose leaned back in her seat and crossed her arms in front of her.

"And Mr. Payton said he would take you to the dance?"

"No." Her answer was almost inaudible. "He said he couldn't be your boyfriend just because I wanted him to be."

"I told you it was a dumb thing to say."

"Rose," Jamie warned, "you're close to losing your TV privileges."

Her older daughter snapped her mouth shut. They'd just gotten a movie on DVD this morning that Rose wanted to see.

"So, Mr. Payton didn't say he would take you and Rose to the dance, did he?"

"No, but he didn't say he wouldn't."

Rose snorted.

"Let's stick with our original plan," Jamie said.

"We'll see," Opal piped up from behind her.

Jamie bit her lip to keep from laughing at how much her daughter's response sounded like her.

"Mom, don't forget the pizza," Rose said as they approached DC's Pizzeria on Route 9.

Jamie flicked her directional. "Don't worry." But she had forgotten, which wasn't like her. She didn't know what was making her so scattered these days. Or did she? Ever since she'd met Eli Payton, her whole life had been a little out of step.

* * *

The kitchen door opened, letting in a blast of cold night air. "Hey." Myles surveyed the pizza boxes. "Did you save any for me?"

Jamie looked up, her gaze bypassing Myles to Eli walking in behind him.

"Mr. Payton brought me home." Myles strode over to the table to more closely inspect the pizza situation.

"So I see." She smiled at Eli, who was still standing by the door, to let him know she wasn't going to light into him again over driving Myles home.

"Want to join us?"

"Thanks, but I just wanted to check on Rose."

"No, stay," Opal prompted. "You can sit next to Mommy." She pointed at the empty seat by Jamie.

Jamie felt her cheeks flush. "Rose is fine. The physician's assistant popped her kneecap right back in place. I wasn't able to this time."

Eli winced, and Jamie bit back a smile.

"Seriously, join us. There's plenty."

Myles's expression questioned that, but she ignored him and moved her chair toward Opal's so Eli could take the seat next to her.

"All right. I'd like that."

"Myles, take Mr. Payton's coat." She eyed her son's coat slung on the back of one of the kitchen chairs. "And hang it and yours up."

He grabbed Eli's ski jacket and hung both on the coat pegs by the door.

Eli sat down and reached over to take a slice of pizza from the box in front of her.

He seemed to take up so much space at the table. She wrapped her ankle around the chair leg and scooted the chair to the right.

"Mommy, you're squishing me."

Jamie's face grew warmer. Maybe Eli would think her cheeks were perpetually rosy.

He placed his pizza on the paper plate Rose had slid over to him and bent his head.

"What are you doing?" Opal asked.

"Giving thanks."

"We don't do that anymore. Mommy said our food comes from the grocery store and not God." The little girl shot a glance at Jamie. "But when we did, my favorite was 'God is great. God is good. So we thank Him for our food. Amen.'"

Jamie braced herself for disapproval. But he looked sad rather than condemning.

"That grace has always been one of my favorites, too," he said.

She nibbled her pizza slice. The prayer had been one of her favorites, at one time. She'd learned it as a child. Jamie placed her pizza on her plate. That she and her kids no longer said grace as a family was her call. But she wasn't going to make an issue of it with Eli. Not in front of the kids. She glanced around the table to see all three of them absorbed in eating their dinner.

Eli caught her gaze, and the lull in conversation became deafening.

She searched her mind for words to fill the silence. Where was Opal's constant chatter when she needed it? "I wanted to thank you for having Sara walk Opal back up the hill. I hated to impose on you and Drew to watch her while I took Rose to Urgent Care."

Eli and Opal shared a silent exchange.

He cleared his throat. "I—"

"Mr. Payton didn't ask Sara to bring me back. I asked her to."

"Did you tell Mr. Payton you were going with Sara?"

Opal pushed her pizza crust around on her plate. "No."

"We've talked about this before. Mr. Payton must have been looking for you."

Eli gave Jamie a curt nod.

"He was probably worried about you."

Opal looked past her to Eli.

"I was concerned and relieved when Drew told me Sara had brought you to your mother."

"Sorry." Opal's gaze dropped back to her plate.

"Apology accepted."

"If you're done with your pizza, you and Rose

should go upstairs and put on your pajamas. Then you can watch the movie."

"Okay." Opal and Rose slipped away.

"I hope Opal didn't give you too much trouble this afternoon."

"No, it was okay."

"Even her pitch to take her to the school dinner-dance?"

"She told you about that?" The smile lines on either side of his mouth deepened.

"Yes. I'm a bit embarrassed," Jamie admitted.

"Don't be. She's what, six? And I'm sure she misses her daddy."

"Seven. Don't let her hear you saying six." *And I'm not sure she misses John as much as she simply misses having a daddy.*

Eli moved his chair back, and a compulsion to make him stay, to not have an empty seat at the table, washed over Jamie.

"Where are my manners? Would you like a drink? We have milk and iced tea. I'm afraid Myles finished off the soda."

Her son pulled his attention from his food. "There wasn't that much left."

"I know." She didn't want the good day and her good mood broken by an argument with Myles. "I could make coffee if you'd rather have something hot."

"Milk is fine."

Jamie rose and crossed the kitchen to the refrigerator.

"I'm going to work on my computer." Myles tossed his paper plate in the trash and put his glass in the sink. "Talk to her about what you told me," he said in a lower voice as he passed by Eli at the table.

"Something I need to know?" Jamie placed Eli's milk in front of him and sat with her tea.

"Thanks." Eli shifted in his seat, and she couldn't get past the similarity of his demeanor and Myles's when he and Tanner were cooking up something.

"I was talking to some of the guys in the youth group about the teen programs at the American Legion."

Jamie tensed. So much for her pleasant day. "I see."

"I told them I would talk with their parents and give them more information."

"Good move. I won't need any more information."

Eli inclined his head. "I understand how, given the circumstances, you might not want Myles involved in an American Legion program."

He had that right. She'd meant it when she'd told him the military had killed John. And she didn't want Myles anywhere near anything or anyone who would encourage him to follow in his father's footsteps. She couldn't lose her son, too.

Eli hesitated as if remembering their last meeting and her displeasure at Myles going to the youth group meeting and Eli driving him home. "As I said, I was talking to the group, not just to Myles."

Jamie was torn between anger at Eli for including Myles in his discussion when he obviously knew her feelings about her son participating in anything military-related, and appreciation of his ready acquiescence to her opposition.

"Sorry I was so short. I know you weren't talking just to Myles." She eyed his empty glass. "Do you want more milk?"

"No, thanks. I should be going." Eli followed Myles's lead and cleared his plate and glass from the table. "Got to be up early for church tomorrow. Speaking of which, I meant to tell you that I'm glad you're letting Myles come to youth group."

Was that a dig? She scanned his face. *No, it was just Eli.* She was so sensitive to everything lately. There were certainly a lot worse things Myles could be doing than going to youth group with Tanner. Her chest tightened. As long as Myles remembered what she'd told him when they'd stopped going to church, to not slip into the complacency of trusting in a higher power that wasn't there. Myles had to learn that he was responsible for himself.

"Thanks, again, for the pizza." He grabbed his coat from the coat pegs by the door and let himself out.

"So, Mom." Myles bounded into the kitchen. He had to have been lurking around the corner in the living room. "Did he tell you?"

"Yes."

"About the rifle class? He's going to be teaching a rifle class." Myles's voice rose in excitement while her heart plummeted. "Did he give you the information and registration form? He had it in his coat pocket."

"We didn't get that far. I told him I didn't need to know more."

"Mo-om! I thought he could talk you into it. I guess it didn't work."

"Mr. Payton knew better than that."

"You're always against me. Now you have Mr. Payton against me. You're at me all of the time to do something constructive. He wants me to get involved in group activities. I come up with something I want to do and you shoot it down."

"I can't let you."

"Dad would have let me," he spat back.

"Your dad…" Her voice cracked. "Is why I can't."

"Doesn't matter. You know I'm going to blow this town and enlist as soon as I'm old enough." He stormed from the room.

She let him go, but not without wishing Eli hadn't gotten Myles going on the course, no matter how good his intentions might have been. Her life had become as up and down as a roller coaster ride since

Eli had entered it. Things might have been better if she could have held on to her initial dislike of him. But the more she saw Eli, the more she liked Eli. To maintain any semblance of tranquility, her best plan might be to avoid him. Her heart tripped. Tranquility might not be all that it was cracked up to be.

Chapter Six

"TGIF," the birthing center office assistant said as she and Jamie left the center. "Autumn joining the midwife practice has taken some of the pressure off Kelly, but it's upped my workload—at least this week."

"You've got that right." After a hectic week with an unusually high number of deliveries at the birthing center, Jamie was more than ready for one of her rare weekends when she wasn't on call.

"Got plans?" the other woman asked.

"Bowling league tonight and nothing else for the rest of the weekend, except shopping with the girls Sunday afternoon. They've both outgrown the shoes they got for school back in August."

The woman laughed as she opened her car door. "Good luck with that. I'm not a shopper and am so glad my daughter is old enough to shop on her own."

Jamie waved goodbye. She was surprised at how

much she was looking forward to bowling again. Soon after she'd first moved to Paradox Lake, Karen Hill had asked her at church one Sunday if she bowled. When Jamie admitted to being on her high school bowling team, Karen had talked her into joining the Friday Fun league she and her husband belonged to.

It had sounded like a good way to get a break from her single-parent role one night a week. She'd hired Neal Hazard's daughter as her regular Friday night babysitter until Autumn had left Paradox Lake to pursue an advanced degree in nursing. Then, Myles had watched the girls for her until she'd found out he was breaking the house rules and having people over when she was out. She'd more or less dropped out of the league last year.

Jamie hummed as she let herself in the house. But now she was back bowling. A call to the bowling alley last week had verified that the league had openings in its winter-spring session that had started last week. And now that Autumn was back in town, she had offered to watch the girls.

She kicked off her nursing clogs and traded her scrubs for a soft pair of well-washed jeans and a turquoise cotton sweater. She hummed to herself as she tied her athletic shoes. For tonight, at least, she could forget her week. Forget the messages Leah had left offering Eli's help in installing the heat valve she'd already installed herself. Forget the call from Leah that Opal had answered when Jamie was working one evening. Opal had explained her idea about Eli taking her and Rose to the dance. Leah had thought that was a great idea and had told Opal she would talk with Eli.

The girls' delighted squeals of "Autumn!" let Jamie know her babysitter had arrived. She bounded down the stairs like one of the kids.

"Hi," she said. "Thanks again for doing this."

"No problem. I've missed these two. I'll keep them busy. Don't worry about a thing."

More likely Opal and Rose would keep Autumn busy. Jamie hesitated. "Jack is coming over to pick up Myles. I hope that isn't a problem. Myles has a part-time job at the garage, starting today."

"It isn't." Autumn's lips curved in a half smile that didn't reach her eyes. "We're still friends, more or less." She chewed her lip. "You were great when he broke up with me before I left for grad school and I needed someone to talk to. Dad didn't understand."

"I'm glad I could help."

"Enough of this old history rehash," Autumn said. "He's married and I've moved on. You don't want to miss warm-up."

"True, it's been a while. I can use some practice throws before the games." Jamie got her coat and bowling bag from the front closet and bundled up to face the frigid night.

She turned to her daughters. "You be good for Autumn."

"We will."

"They can stay up until nine. You can make them popcorn if you want."

"Will do. Now, go." Autumn waved her off. "It's not like I haven't done this before."

"All right. I'm going."

Jamie's stomach flip-flopped most of the twenty-minute drive to Ticonderoga. She couldn't figure out why she was nervous. She'd bowled with these people before. She dropped her hand to her stomach. She probably should have had eaten more than the protein bar she'd grabbed for supper when she'd gotten home. The kids had already demolished the mac and cheese she'd left for Myles to heat up for them, and it had been too late to make anything else.

The parking lot of the bowling alley was already half full when she pulled in. She got out and hauled her bowling bag from the passenger-side seat. The flutter started again.

"Jamie, we're over here," Karen called and waved when she got inside.

Several other people greeted her as she walked to lane ten.

"Good to see you back," Tom Hill said. "Practice will start in a minute."

Jamie sat and put her bowling shoes on. She placed her ball on the return rack. "Tom, I want to thank you again for giving Myles a job. He's set his mind on buying back John's Miata."

"We can use the help, and he seems willing to learn. As for the car, Jack's looking to sell it." He shrugged and grinned. "You know, with the baby coming and all."

"No, I didn't know."

"That's right. You weren't at church," Karen said. "He and Suzy announced it last week."

A pang of regret struck Jamie at Karen's matter-of-fact statement, as if Jamie might have been at church, hadn't stopped going months ago.

"Congratulations to everyone."

"Thanks," the expectant grandparents said.

Jamie stood. "I might as well give it a go." She lifted her ball, sighted it with the head pin, took her four steps and let it rip.

The pins flew with a resounding crash, reminding her of how, after John's death, she'd projected her anger at him, the war, God and the world at large onto the pins. It had helped, in a fashion.

The last pin standing wobbled and fell. *A strike.*

Karen and Tom clapped.

"Nice ball."

It couldn't be. Jamie spun around.

"Do you know Eli Payton?" Karen asked. "He's our fourth."

Jamie swallowed. "Yes, he's Myles's guidance counselor."

"Then I don't have to make introductions," Karen said.

"No, no need," Jamie said, wondering if her clipped words sounded as rude to her teammates as they did to her. But bowling was her getaway from life's problems. And Eli Payton had every sign of proving to be a problem. "I need to get something to eat. Do any of you want me to order you something?"

Tom looked over at the line by the snack bar. "You'll miss the rest of practice."

"I have a feeling I won't need it." *All I'll have to do is think of Eli and Myles and the rifle course at the American Legion that Myles is still bugging me about.*

Eli watched Jamie weave her way across the bowling alley. She must not have asked who the fourth team member was. He hoped it wouldn't matter. When Karen had told him Jamie was going to join their team, he'd thought it would be fun to spend some time with her socially rather than as Myles's guidance counselor.

"You ditching practice, too?" Tom asked, eyeing the score sheet with their averages on the table behind him.

"The way I bowled last week, I'd better not."

"You've got that right."

Eli stepped down to the lane. Tom was a serious bowler. Eli enjoyed the sport, win or lose. He took his shot and hit the head pin dead-on, leaving a pin standing in the back row on either side of the lane—a seven-ten split. He moved aside to let the next bowler take the pickup shot.

Tom waved him back. "You need practice on this shot more than I do."

All right. He had shot more than his share of splits last week. Tom didn't have to remind him. He stepped up and put exactly the right curve on the ball so that it struck the ten pin on the right side and kicked it to the left. Eli held his breath. Not enough. The ten pin rolled back off the lane without hitting the seven.

"Wow! I thought you had it." Jamie placed her cheeseburger and drink on the table overlooking the lane.

Tom cut short Eli's enjoyment of Jamie's compliment. "You should have gotten behind it more."

Eli bristled. "I know." He didn't need Tom telling him how to bowl. Or was it that he didn't need Tom telling him how to bowl in front of Jamie?

The sixty-second countdown to the end of practice ticked off.

"You've got time for another ball," Tom urged.

Eli glanced back at Jamie, who was engrossed in

her burger, before stepping to the line. He sighted his ball and threw. Another split. The counter hit zero, signaling the end of practice.

"Too fast," Tom said.

Eli frowned at the ball return. Tom's helpful advice might make for a long night.

"Jamie, I have you up first," Karen said.

She put her food down and wiped her hands with a wet wipe she'd found in her bag and dried them with a napkin. Then she picked up her ball and with a smooth, graceful delivery, she shot a strike.

"Way to go!" Eli boomed, moving to the edge of the molded plastic seat. He stopped himself from leaping up when he saw the members of the other team looking at him. Hey, there was nothing wrong with cheering on a teammate.

Jamie turned and beamed at him. Well, at everyone. And his heart skipped a beat.

"Nice one," Karen said.

Tom gave her a high five.

Eli rose for his turn. He felt Jamie's eyes on him as he bent to lift his ball and grabbed the towel instead. He wiped his hand and held it over the fan for a couple of seconds before picking up the ball. Taking a deep breath and releasing it, he shot. The ball curved directly toward the head pin, and his spirits sank as he waited for the split. With a loud crash, the pins all flew down. A strike.

Tom patted his back as he sat. "Just like I told you to do."

Behind him, the rattle of ice in a cup didn't quite muffle a distinctive snort.

The second through eighth frames were more of the same. Jamie and Eli shot strikes. On the ninth frame the bowling alley went quiet when Jamie rose for her turn. She aimed, took two steps of her approach and stopped. She started over. Eli held his breath as her perfect-looking ball left the seven-pin standing.

A collective "Aw" rolled through the bowling alley.

"It's still the best game I've ever bowled," she said as she waited for her ball to return.

"You can pick it up," Eli said, surprised at how confident he was she would and how much he wanted her to.

She lifted her ball to him and smiled. He relaxed back in his seat and watched her throw the spare.

"Nice one," one of the guys on the other team said before Eli could. Eli's jaw tightened when she smiled at the guy.

"Your turn," Tom said as he finished his frame.

Again the lanes turned nerve-rackingly quiet. Nothing like pouring on the pressure. What did it matter? He didn't have to get a strike. He was a twenty-first-century guy. He didn't need to beat

Jamie. But a voice in the back of his head said, "You'd like to impress her."

As soon as he released his ball, he knew it was off. The center pins fell, leaving the ten-pin standing and seven pin wobbling. He grabbed the towel and dried his hands. When he turned back, the seven had fallen. Not his best side, but he could pick off the seven a whole lot easier than he could have aced the split. He took his best shot and closed his eyes like a novice bowler until he heard the impact.

"Good work," Tom said. "You didn't let her get ahead."

Karen and Jamie skewered him from either side with razor-sharp glares.

"What?" Tom asked.

The comedy of it drained the tension that had been building in Eli. Part of him had the same fervor to beat Jamie that Tom had expressed. The other part wanted to simply enjoy the competition.

As Jamie readied herself for the first ball of the tenth frame, someone slurred, "You can do it, honey," from the vicinity of the bar.

Eli half rose to locate the speaker and tell him to be quiet.

Tom touched his arm. "It's not worth it."

Eli started to say he was just stretching. "You're right. But I don't have to like it."

"Well, you'd better get used to it. Jamie is a very attractive woman."

Eli realized that this was the first time he'd agreed with Tom all night.

The crack of pins pulled Eli's attention back to Jamie. She'd thrown another strike. He leaped up and cheered, not caring who saw or what—he glanced sideways at Tom—they might think. Jamie was his teammate.

Her next ball left two pins standing. He held his hands in his lap and closed his eyes as she released her last shot.

"Praying for her to spare or miss?" Tom asked.

"Neither." Eli frowned at him and caught Jamie's shot knocking down one pin and leaving the other standing.

She turned and jumped up and down clapping. "I can't believe it. Wait until I tell the kids my score." Both teams gathered around Jamie to congratulate her.

Eli measured whether he could slip by them and quietly finish his game. He slid from the chair.

"Eli, sorry." Jamie moved off the lane, excitement still radiating from her in waves. "I got carried away. I've never bowled like that before."

"Enjoy it. You bowled a great game."

She accepted the hand he offered in congratulations and he marveled at how small and soft hers felt in his. Too soon, she finished the handshake and let go of his hand. "Now, let's see what you can do."

He breathed deeply through his nose and blew his breath out his mouth to relax his tensed muscles. This was ridiculous. It was only a game, not even a competitive game. He lifted his ball from the return and weighed it in his hands. *It's only a game.* He made his approach and threw. The ball rolled off his hand and spun directly toward the right pocket and right by it to hit the headpin. He didn't have to wait until the pins cleared. A seven-ten split.

"Tough luck," Tom said.

Eli frowned. It wasn't as if he'd never made this spare. He had. Once. He could again. Or, he could pick off the seven pin and leave it a tie. He grabbed his ball. Might as well get it over with.

His approach was smooth. The ball hugged the right gutter causing a gasp from somewhere behind him and veered toward the left as it reached the ten pin. With a crack, the pin flew to the left, landed shy of the seven pin and spun around to knock it down.

"You did it!" Jamie's voice rose above the others.

He turned. She grinned.

He admired her sportsmanship. "But I beat you."

"We're teammates. It's the overall pins that count. And, I don't know about you, but I think we're going to need some more help from our other teammates next week." She looked directly at Tom.

Eli concentrated on picking up his ball from the return to hide the grin on his face.

"I know I can't be counted on to duplicate tonight every week," Jamie said.

He got his mirth under control. "Me neither."

"Yeah, yeah," Tom said. "Knock it off. I knew you were going to pick up the spare. I was encouraging you."

"Right! And if I encouraged the students who come into the guidance office that way, the district would see an uptick in its dropout rate."

Tom laughed and slapped him on the back.

"Nice game." Several of the other bowlers interrupted their good-natured banter to congratulate Jamie and Eli.

"You two are good together," one of their opposing team members said.

Eli gazed over at Jamie talking with Karen. They were good together. But apparently only when there were no kids involved and the conversation didn't veer to anything church-or military-related.

Jamie rose and reached for her coat. She'd had a really nice time tonight, and it wasn't only the exhilaration of bowling her best game ever. It was the company, too, including Eli. She hadn't even had to project his face on the pins.

"Got a minute?" he asked. "The snack bar is still open. We could have a celebratory soda or hot chocolate."

"I can't. I have to pick up Myles, and I told the sitter I'd be back before ten."

He checked his watch. "Okay."

Did she detect a note of disappointment in his voice?

"Then what time do you want me to come over tomorrow?"

"Excuse me?"

He picked up her ball bag for her. "To work on your heating system."

She reached for the bag.

"I'll carry it out to your car. Mom said Saturday was a good day to come over."

Opal. It had to have been the conversation she'd had with Leah.

His eyes lit with understanding. "You didn't talk with my mother. You don't need my help."

"No, but Opal talked with your mother."

He nodded. "Uh-huh."

"Thanks anyway. Myles and I already replaced the valve."

"And I assume you didn't ask my mother to ask me to reconsider taking the girls to their dinner-dance at school?"

"No." They walked to the door. She pushed it open and held it for him, since his hands were full.

He pressed his shoulder against the door as if to let her enter first.

"Go ahead."

He hesitated, then moved around her, filling the doorway. They stepped into the cold night air.

"I can't believe her." He strode across the front of the parking lot to her vehicle parked at the far end of the building. "I cancelled my usual Saturday morning workout with the trainer at the gym because Mom said she'd promised you."

She unlocked the door. "Promised Opal is more likely. I'm sure your mother meant well." Jamie reached to take her bowling bag from Eli.

"I know." He handed it over, opened the back door and leaned against the back quarter panel.

She put the bag on the floor. "If you're in need of something to do, you could come over and help Myles and me lay fiberglass insulation in the attic."

"I could do that. What time do you want me there?"

Jamie straightened. "I was kind of kidding."

He pushed away from the vehicle. "I'm almost as good at laying insulation as I am at heating repairs."

She laughed. "Why don't you come over about nine?"

"I'll be there." He whistled as he walked back up the line of cars to his double-cab truck.

Jamie climbed into her vehicle and stared at the giant bowling pin painted on the side of the bowling alley. Had she really just invited Eli over to her house for the day?

Chapter Seven

At the sound of the car pulling in to the driveway, Scooby started barking and raced to the door. Jamie glanced at her watch. Nine o'clock. Eli was right on time, not that she'd expect otherwise. She stopped in front of the mirror on the dining room wall, fluffed her hair and smoothed her soft lavender-colored sweater over her favorite jeans.

"Did you forget to comb your hair?" Opal asked, coming up behind her.

"No." She'd not only washed and blow-dried her hair, she'd also put on makeup and her favorite earrings. No harm in looking nice, even if she wasn't going anywhere special.

Rose looked up from the cereal she was finishing. "You look pretty."

"Thanks, sweetie."

"Mommy!" Opal called from the living room. "It's Mr. Payton."

"Remember what we talked about," Jamie warned.

She'd discussed Eli's coming over with her daughter at breakfast and laid down the law about Opal not bothering Eli to take her and Rose to the dinner-dance. Opal had cheerfully agreed, while spooning down two bowls of her favorite cereal, rousing suspicion that the child hadn't heard a word she'd said.

The house phone rang as she started toward the living room. She picked it up from the sideboard and checked the caller ID. It was Rose's scout leader. "Hello."

"Jamie? I'm glad I caught you before you left. Could you pick Katy up on your way over? Her dad's car won't start."

"No problem. I'm trying to get the girls going now."

"Thanks. See you in a bit."

"Bye." Jamie carried the phone to the living room to put it back in the charger.

"She's in the other room fixing her hair." Opal's voice carried into the dining room. "She put on her date-night earrings."

Jamie stopped in the doorway and touched her right earlobe. What had possessed her to put on the sapphire earrings John had given her for their twelfth anniversary, the last they'd had together? She was going to spend the day insulating the attic.

Opal chattered on. "And mascara and the sweater

we gave her for Christmas. It's the first time she's worn it."

"Opal."

The little girl jerked her head around. "What? I'm not bothering Mr. Payton about taking me to the dance. And Rose told me those were your date-night earrings. I was just telling Mr. Payton."

Eli's facial muscles worked, as if he was struggling to contain his grin.

"Go tell your brother Mr. Payton is here to start the attic. And you and Rose need to get ready."

Opal dragged herself from the room.

"I'll take your coat." She took his ski jacket, ignoring the glint of humor in his eyes, and hung it in the closet. "Myles should be right down. I need to run Rose and Opal over to Rose's scout leader's house."

Jamie turned to see the glint dim. It looked like her comment about leaving had quashed any idea he might have gotten from Opal that she'd dressed up for him, even if she subconsciously had.

"Rose's troop is going to a program at Fort Ticonderoga as part of their history badge, and they're letting Opal tag along."

"So it's just Myles and me."

Did she detect a note of disappointment in his voice? *No.* They'd had a good time bowling last night, but that didn't mean anything. Her mind drifted to the smooth, athletic way he bowled. Eli and Myles working together without her might not be a bad idea. It would give Myles some constructive male time. But what would she do all day?

And you wouldn't be being honest with Eli if you let him think you have something else to do when you don't.

Do not steal. Do not lie. Do not deceive one another. Leviticus 19:11 played in her head. She mentally stored it back in the recesses of her mind where she'd banished all of her Bible learning when she'd stopped going to church.

"You can't get rid of me that easily. I'll be back in a half hour or so."

"Take as long as you need. We should be able to hold down the fort until you get back." He glanced over her shoulder.

"Hi, Mr. Payton." Myles came down the stairs two at a time followed by Opal.

"Myles."

"Want a cup of coffee or something?" Myles asked. "I haven't had breakfast." He glanced at her. "You did make coffee, didn't you, Mom?"

"Yes, I made coffee." He son had recently taken to drinking coffee in the morning. She didn't know if he enjoyed it or thought it made him seem more grown-up.

"Coffee sounds good." Eli shot her a warm smile before allowing Myles to lead him from the room.

"Mommy." Opal tugged her hand, and Jamie

realized she was staring at the empty doorway. "Are we going or what?"

"Yes. Go see what's keeping your sister."

"Go here. Go there. I already got Myles for you," Opal complained as she went to get Rose.

"I'll be outside warming the car up," Jamie called after her.

An hour later, she let herself back in the house. Stopping at the Paradox Lake General Store on her way home had taken longer than she'd expected. She put the ham and cheese she'd bought for lunch in the refrigerator, pausing to listen to the heavy footsteps overhead. What was it that made boys so loud?

Jamie closed the refrigerator and headed up to join them. As she reached the top of the stairs, the strains of a song by Myles's favorite band drifted down from the attic. She ducked into her room and exchanged her sweater for an old sweatshirt that was more appropriate for home repairs. She fingered one of her earrings before taking them out and putting them in her jewelry box.

It was foolish to have worn them in the first place. Jamie drew in a deep, pained breath. She'd never forgive herself if she'd lost one. They were John's last gift to her. But they'd gone so well with her sweater. The sweater she'd worn to look nice for Eli. What had she been thinking? Jamie shook her head. She hadn't been thinking, not with her head. She was a healthy thirty-four-year-old woman who'd wanted to look nice for a man. Her throat clogged. A man other than John. A man she wasn't even sure she liked.

The ladder steps to the attic creaked as she climbed them. When she reached the top and poked her head through the trapdoor opening in the floor, she found Eli alone rolling insulation down the peaked ceiling.

"Hi." She cleared her throat. "Where's Myles?"

Eli stapled the insulation to the top joist. "Over at Hill's."

Jamie ground her teeth. He'd ditched his work to go tinker with that old car? And Eli had let him? That didn't seem right.

Eli stepped back to the middle of the room where he could just barely stand straight. "Tom called. He needed help at the shop. Jack was supposed work today, but Suzy wasn't feeling well and he took her to the birthing center."

"Oh, no. I hope everything is okay." She hauled herself up into the attic.

"Karen is in charge of the Community Church prayer chain, and she has the calls going out."

Jamie studied her hands. "I suppose some people can take solace in that." But not her. Not anymore.

"And more." His voice was soft, but firm.

She ignored Eli's implied reference to a higher power she no longer believed in. "Kelly and Autumn have appointments today. Suzy will be in good hands."

"The best."

Jamie knew he didn't mean the two midwives. "What do you need me to do?" She motioned to the insulation.

"I'll hold and feed you the roll, and you can staple the insulation to the joists."

Halfway across the room, her phone chimed a text. "I need to check this. It could be the center, even though I'm not supposed to be on call."

She looked at the lit screen. It wasn't the center. It was from Myles. Did Mr. Payton talk to you? What do you think?

Her stomach tightened. Myles wasn't still trying to get her to change her mind about the American Legion rifle class, was he?

She eyed Eli, hoping he wasn't encouraging Myles. She'd been clear to both of them. "It's from Myles. Something about your talking with me."

His eyes darkened.

She might as well get it right out. "If this is about the rifle course at the American Legion, Myles is sorely mistaken if he thinks you can convince me to change my mind."

Eli let the insulation drop and hang from the ceiling. "That's not what we were talking about." He shoved his hands into the front pockets of his jeans. "Pastor Joel is starting a confirmation class. Some of the kids at youth group were talking about it. Myles asked me to talk to you about letting him sign up for it."

Jamie curled her fingers until her nails dug into her palms. She had joined her parents' church when she was Myles's age. "I don't…" She stopped. Maybe the best way to protect Myles from falling into the same dependency on faith that had failed her was for him to learn more about religious tenets so he could recognize the cold hard reality.

She breathed in the warm, dusty attic air. "I don't see why not."

Eli blinked away his stare. "That's great. Joel has a super program worked out. I think Myles and the other kids will get a lot out of it. There's even a parents' module, so you can see what the kids are learning."

"That's probably good." She was pleased that she was able to keep her words even and emotion free. "You wanted me to staple the insulation?"

"Yeah." He pulled his hands from his pockets and looked over at the dangling insulation.

She took the opportunity to pick up the stapler while his gaze was elsewhere and he couldn't see her hand shaking.

Eli pushed the insulation against the wall and held it as he watched Jamie bend to pick up the stapler. He ran his gaze over her unruly curls and down the straight line of her back. She'd changed from the pretty sweater she'd had on earlier to a baggy blue sweatshirt with a Buffalo Bills emblem on the front.

She looked up and caught him staring at her. He rubbed the back of his neck. "So, I don't have to ask who you'll be favoring in the game tomorrow."

She blinked.

"The Bills-Patriots game."

"The sweatshirt. My dad gave it to me years ago. I grew up in Western New York. There's some kind of unwritten code that if you're born there, you have to support the Bills for your whole life no matter where you live. It was tough at a couple of bases where we were posted."

Posted. With her husband. Who'd probably been a Bills fan, too. Which for some reason bothered him.

"How about you? A Giants fan?" A lot of the people in Eastern New York were.

"Nope."

"Not the Patriots?"

"Yep." He wasn't a die-hard Patriots fan, but since the Bills and the Patriots were longtime rivals and he suspected she was more of a Bills fan than she was letting on, he couldn't resist aligning himself with the Pats. To see her reaction if nothing else.

"And after bowling last night I thought we were finally starting to get along." The light dancing in her eyes ruined the stern expression she was struggling to maintain.

"It would have been better if I'd said the Giants or Jets?"

"Minimally."

"Hey, do you want to catch the game tomorrow? I have a sixty-inch-screen TV."

She rubbed the palms of her hands down the front of her jeans and stared at the floor.

Swift. He'd said the wrong thing again, and she was trying to come up with a nice way of saying no.

"I promised Rose and Opal I'd take them shopping tomorrow afternoon." The light danced in her eyes again. "I'm recording the game to watch when I get home."

He knew it. He knew she wasn't a casual fan.

"Myles is going over to Tanner's to study. I've told him not to tell me anything about the game if they watch it."

"You don't have to explain."

"Explain what?" She held the stapler as if she were ready to defend herself.

He was suffering from a bad case of foot in mouth. She hadn't told him where Myles would be while she was out with the girls because she was expecting him to ask. She was just making conversation. He should know better than to try to second-guess a woman's thoughts and motivations. If he didn't change his tactics fast, the collateral damage could prove insurmountable.

"Yourself. Anything. We should get to work if we're going to finish this job today." He breathed easier when Jamie chose to dismiss his comment with a sidelong glance.

She closed the space between them. He pressed the insulation against the wall, and she rose on her tiptoes between his arms and reached up to staple it. The fresh fragrance of her hair tickled his nose and cut through the mustiness that permeated the attic.

With a click from the stapler, she securely fastened the batting and ducked out from under his arms, leaving a cool emptiness between him and the slanted ceiling.

"I can finish this," she said, "if you want to go ahead and measure and cut the next strip."

"Sure." Putting some space between them might be a good idea. The attic didn't seem nearly as cavernous with Jamie helping as it had when he'd first come up with Myles.

He watched her neatly staple the insulation down the wall at four-inch intervals.

She stood. "You were going to cut the next strip."

"Right." He unhooked the measuring tape from his back pocket. "I wanted to make sure you didn't need any help."

Hands on hips, she smiled and shook her head.

"I was admiring your work." *And how cute you looked doing it.*

"Better," she said. "This isn't the first time I've installed insulation."

"Duly noted. I'd better watch my work, or I might be out of a job."

"I think you're safe until Myles gets back. Did he say when he'd be done at the garage?"

"No." Eli unrolled the next batt, knowing that Jamie was watching him, and expertly cut it to length. After her reluctance last night to accept his offer of help, he'd had second thoughts about coming over this morning. Obviously, she and Myles could have handled the job without him. But now he had a feeling the day might turn out to be enjoyable. He looked up at Jamie's heart-shaped face. Very enjoyable.

Jamie wiped her forearm across her forehead. "What do you say we take a break and have some lunch? It must be time." Her stomach growled in agreement.

"I'm with you there." He looked around. "Not bad. We should be able to finish this afternoon."

"What do you mean not bad? Myles and I would have never gotten this much done."

"You're right." He grinned and motioned to the opening to the stair ladder. "After you."

Jamie hesitated. "Could you go first? It's silly. I'm fine coming up the steps, but I like to have someone hold the ladder when I go down."

Eli raised an eyebrow. She should go ahead and climb down, but her feet didn't seem to want to cooperate.

"It's just that I fell off a ladder when I was little. Or more precisely, I fell with the ladder when it tipped over. I wasn't supposed to be on it. Dad had looked away for a minute. I sprained my wrist and broke my leg."

A sympathetic smile softened his features. "A little impetuous, were you?"

"Sort of like Opal."

His eyes lit with amusement.

"Okay, a lot like Opal. So are you going to humor me and hold the ladder or not?"

"There's nothing I'd rather do." He lowered himself through the floor, filling the square cutout with his broad, T-shirt clad shoulders. Until now, she hadn't realized how warm she'd gotten working. Maybe she should change into a T-shirt, too, before they came back up to finish.

"All clear."

Jamie reached for the first step with her right foot and planted her hands firmly on the floor for balance. Her cheeks heated as she realized the view she must be giving Eli. *Too late now.* As her head cleared the ceiling, she looked over her shoulder into Eli's smoky eyes. With his hands on either side of the stairs frame, he had her boxed in like he had upstairs before he'd backed off and let her staple the insulation by herself.

Her foot reached for the floor and Eli placed his hand on the small of her back for support.

She turned and smiled. "I'm down."

Eli stood motionless, staring at her, his hand still on her back. Her stomach quivered.

"Right." He shoved away and the quiver stilled to emptiness.

Jamie brushed an errant curl back from her face. "I'm fine with the regular stairs," she said to fill the growing silence. "I mean I can go first." She scuffed her sneaker against the hardwood floor. She was blathering.

"Hey, it's okay. We all have our insecurities."

"I guess." Jamie took in his sympathetic yet take-charge manner and wondered what his could be.

"I'll wash up and run out for sandwiches for us at the General Store."

"You'll need to clean up downstairs. There's no bath up here. And I stopped and bought ham and cheese for sandwiches on my way back from dropping off Rose and Opal."

"Great. I'm starved. Tell you what. In return, I'll buy you the cheeseburger special at bowling next Friday."

"You don't have to." The thought of him buying her dinner, even at the lanes, unsettled her. It wasn't like he had to pay her back.

"I don't have to… I want to."

Eli's correction revived the quiver in her stomach. It was silly. She'd simply enjoyed working with someone who seemed to like home improvement work as much as she did. Someone who wasn't in a rush to get it done and over with like Myles. Or, she had to admit it, like John had been. That's all. There was no need to let herself be bothered about it.

"Okay." She relented. "A cheeseburger special on Friday. Let's get washed up. All of this talk of food has me starved now, too."

Jamie led him down into the living room, catching her reflection in the mirror decorating the wall next to the open stairway. She ran her hand over her hair. The humidity in the attic had turned it into a tousled riot of curls.

"Hi, Mommy!" Opal greeted them from the front doorway.

Jamie stopped in mid-step and Eli almost crashed into her. Her gaze flew to the clock on the DVR. She hadn't been keeping track of time. Her first thought was that she'd missed the girls' pick-up time, which wasn't like her. *No, it was only one fifteen.* She wasn't supposed to pick them up for another hour. She placed her hand on her chest. She hadn't given the girls a thought all morning.

"Hi, sweetie. Is everything okay?" Jamie descended the last three stairs. She looked past Opal for Rose, afraid her knee might have kicked out again. Rose had chaffed about taking it easy as the PA had instructed.

"Everything's fine." Charlotte Russell followed Opal in with her daughter, Katy, and Rose. "The presentation at the Fort was shorter than expected. Sonja called all of the parents but didn't get an answer here."

"She must have called the house phone. We were in the attic putting up insulation."

"I see." Charlotte's gaze moved from Jamie to Eli.

Jamie's heart dropped. Charlotte Russell was one of the biggest gossips in Essex County. She hated to think what the woman might be making of her not answering the phone and walking down the stairs with Eli looking somewhat disheveled. Jamie had always thought privately that Charlotte was unhappy in her life and wanted others to be as miserable as she was. Let Charlotte think whatever she wanted to think. Jamie looked up at the ceiling. *But please don't let her share it.*

"Since you picked up Katy this morning when her father's car wouldn't start, I figured I'd bring the girls." Charlotte's reference to her estranged husband dripped with distaste.

"Thanks."

Opal broke the silence that enveloped the room. "This is Mommy's friend Mr. Payton. He likes to come over and help us with things."

Jamie cringed. Opal was not helping the situation.

"I know Mr. Payton." If the silence in the room a minute ago was disconcerting, the chill that had taken its place was almost paralyzing.

"Charlie." Eli used a nickname Jamie hadn't heard anyone else use.

"Eli."

Jamie realized that Eli hadn't moved from his place halfway up the stairs. There was definitely some history between the two.

"Thanks again for bringing Rose and Opal home."

"Yes, we'd better get going."

"But, Mom," her daughter Katy said. "I thought you were going to check with Rose's mother about letting me stay here while you go grocery shopping. I hate grocery shopping."

"I'm sure it's okay," Rose said. "Right, Mom?"

"Not today." Charlotte turned Katy toward the door and hustled her out.

Jamie had a sinking feeling not any other day, either, as long as she and Eli were friends.

Eli pounded down the stairs, a vein pulsing in his temple. He faced Rose and Jamie. "I'm sorry."

The little girl looked at him then at her mother and scratched her cheek.

"For spoiling your plans."

Rose tilted her head to one side and pursed her lips.

He wasn't any better at talking with Rose than

he was at talking with her mother. But—he thought about their bowling match and installing the insulation—he and Jamie did work well together. Maybe he should just avoid talking.

"Are you hungry?" Jamie asked with a forced cheerfulness that, from the looks on their faces, didn't fool Rose and Opal any more than it fooled him. "I know you had lunch at the fort, but I bought your favorite cookies this morning. There's one for each of you in the bakery box in the upper cupboard." She gave the doorway to the dining room a pointed look.

"Okay. Come on, Opal." Rose shot Jamie a befuddled look.

"I'm sorry about that." Eli repeated himself. "Old bad feelings." Feelings he'd thought he'd moved past.

Jamie bit her lip and nodded. "I need to see to the girls. The bath is down the hall. I can clean up in the kitchen."

Jamie's apparent need to put some space between them cut him. He took his time walking down the hall. He'd forgiven Charlie for her lies. But when he'd seen the look of panic on Jamie's face and Rose's disappointment, he'd almost lost it. It had taken all of his control not to physically remove Charlie from Jamie's house. Fortunately, with some help from above, his rational side had prevailed.

Eli turned the water on full force and lathered his

hands. Charlie could be vindictive and, according to his mother, she was a terrible gossip. The last thing he wanted was for Charlie to shred Jamie's reputation to get back at him. He'd done a lot of things he wasn't proud of when he was a teen but not what Charlie had accused him of. He shut off the hot water and splashed cold on his face. It didn't even begin to cool him down. He dried his hands and face and mentally armed himself to face Jamie. When he'd returned to Paradox Lake, he'd prayed that his past would remain in the past.

"Mr. Payton." Opal skipped up the hall to him. "I made you a sandwich. All by myself. Right here." She motioned to the table as they entered the kitchen. "You can sit by me." She hopped up on a chair.

Eli's gaze went to Jamie. Her back to the table and him, she busied herself wiping down the counter in short, fast swipes.

"Come on," Opal urged. "Try your sandwich."

Still focused on Jamie, Eli took the seat next to Opal.

"It's ham and cheese with special sauce," she said.

He bowed his head in a quick blessing before lifting the sandwich to his mouth.

"Mr. Payton is saying grace before he eats like we used to," Opal informed Rose in a loud whisper.

Jamie slapped the sponge against the counter.

Each swipe emphasized the spiritual gap between

them, the same kind of gap that had hastened his and his former fiancée's breakup. He bit into his sandwich, chewing without tasting. "Special sauce, you say?"

Opal nodded. "I made up the recipe myself."

"It's mustard and mayonnaise," Rose said.

"You're not supposed to tell. It's my secret recipe."

Rose rolled her eyes.

"I won't tell." Eli looked back at Jamie, who was wringing out the sponge so hard he expected her to tear it in half. "Aren't you going to join us?"

She placed the sponge on the back of the sink in a precise line with the corner. "I'm not very hungry."

"After all the hard work we did upstairs, you're not hungry?" he teased.

She exhaled. "A glass of milk will be fine." She walked to the seat opposite him and filled the glass sitting at that place with milk.

"I already poured your milk," Opal pointed at the glass in front of Eli.

"Thanks." He hadn't even noticed it.

Jamie sipped her drink. "Did you have a good time at the fort?"

"Yes!" Rose said. "We got to go on a special tour, not the lame one we went on with school."

Jamie focused completely on Rose as the little girl relayed her morning detail by detail. And Eli focused on Jamie. The stiff way she held herself.

The smile that didn't reach her eyes when she commented on Rose's description of the morning. His anger simmered, whether still at Charlie or at the undercurrent of blame he felt from the way Jamie was acting he wasn't sure. He and Jamie hadn't done anything wrong.

He washed the last of his sandwich down with milk. "I'd better get back to work." He pushed his chair back and rose.

"You really don't need to." Jamie ran her finger up and down her empty milk tumbler. "I mean, we made such good progress this morning. I'm sure Myles and I can finish it. You probably have other things you want to do today."

The camaraderie they'd shared this morning had vanished like the morning mist on the mountains on a hot July day.

"I could finish it myself this afternoon."

"No, really, Myles and I can do it." Jamie's gaze flitted from him to Rose to Opal and back to him.

He took that to mean end of discussion. "I'll be going, then."

"Doesn't Mr. Payton get a cookie?" Opal asked.

He didn't have much of a sweet tooth, but it would buy him more time with Jamie.

She drew her lips into a thin line.

"No, not today. That will leave more for you and your sister." He winked and Opal giggled.

"Bye, Mr. Payton," Opal and Rose said.

"Bye."

"I'll get your coat." Jamie walked him to the door. "Thanks for all of your help." She handed him his jacket.

He pulled it on and shifted his weight from one foot to the other. "See you Friday. Bowling."

"Yeah, if I can make it. With kids, you never know what will come up."

As he walked to his truck, he had a gut feeling that something would come up, which bothered him more than it should.

Chapter Eight

"Nice work, Mom." Myles slammed his backpack on the floor, startling Jamie so that she almost dropped the basket of laundry she was carrying.

"Hey," she said sharply before she saw the pain in his eyes and the tear in the pocket of his coat. She put the basket on the table and softened her voice. "What?"

"The kids at school were talking about Mr. Payton's new girlfriend. *You!* They were all looking at me in the hall. Don't you ever think about anyone but yourself?" Myles pushed by her.

She grabbed his arm. "Stop right there. You're upset, but that doesn't give you the right to yell at me. Do you want to talk about it?" She was sure *all* of the kids weren't talking about them. But someone must have said something that had really gotten to Myles.

He pulled away from her. "What's there to talk

about? You and Mr. Payton are having a thing and I didn't even know it. You're such a hypocrite, sneaking around behind my back. I had to slug Liam Russell for some of the stuff he implied about you."

Charlotte's son. If Myles weren't so upset and his words hadn't tied her stomach in knots, she could have smiled at his paternalistic outrage.

"Sit down. Now. Please."

He grabbed a chair, threw himself into it and glared at her. "Don't worry. You're not going to get a call about me fighting. The other guys broke it up before anyone saw us."

She pulled out the chair next to him and sat. "Get this straight. Mr. Payton and I aren't having a thing. We aren't sneaking around on anyone."

"That's not what Liam said."

The knot in her stomach tightened. Myles was going to believe a kid at school over her? Of course he was. Myles was a fourteen-year-old boy, and Charlotte's son Liam was a senior and the school's star athlete.

"He said his mother brought Rose and Opal home and you and Mr. Payton came down from upstairs looking all guilty when you heard them come in."

She crossed her arms. "His mother told him that?"

"No, he heard her talking on the phone."

Terrific! The whole town probably knew by now.

"Mr. Payton and I were insulating the attic. You knew that."

Myles avoided her gaze. "You left the bowling alley with him Friday night. They all saw you."

Jamie had no idea who "they" were or that so many people were interested in her every move. "Eli walked me to the car. We're on the same team with Karen and Tom Hill."

Myles pounded the table with his fist. "What about Dad? Have you forgotten all about him?"

So, that's what was at the bottom of this. She could worry about the gossip Charlotte was spreading about her later. Her baby was hurting.

She reached over and put her hand on top of his. "I know you miss your dad. I miss him, too."

He shook off her hand. "Yeah, right. Mr. Payton isn't half the man Dad was. You know Liam's older brother, Brett? Mr. Payton is his father but he won't own up to it. Liam said so."

"Stop! You don't know that's true."

Eli wouldn't abandon a child, although he wouldn't have been much more than a child himself when Brett was born. And a pretty wild one from what he'd said. No, if nothing else, Leah Summers would have made him take responsibility for his actions. Unless that's why he joined the Air Force. He'd said the service had saved him. Was that what he'd been saved from? It would explain the tension between him and Charlotte on Saturday. Her thoughts ricocheted off each other, threatening to explode into a killer headache.

"And you don't know it's not true. I can tell by the way you're thinking about it."

"Enough!" She stood and shoved the clothes basket across the table to him. "Put your laundry away. I have to go pick up Rose and Opal from Girl Scouts. We can talk when I get back."

"How do you know I'll be here when you get back?"

She didn't. She breathed in deeply. "Because I trust you to be here."

"Fine." He grabbed the basket and left the room.

She'd count that as one for her side.

Jamie bundled up and stepped out onto the porch. Sleet stung her cheeks. It looked like the January thaw they'd been enjoying was over, as if she didn't have enough on her mind without the weather turning on her. She gritted her teeth and walked gingerly down the iced-over sidewalk to her vehicle. She knew how to drive well enough in icy winter weather, but she didn't have to like it.

As she approached the end of the driveway, she heard the humming, scraping sound of the snowplow spreading salt on the road. She loosened her grip on the steering wheel and pulled out behind the plow, wishing she'd bought the new tires the crossover needed with her last paycheck, rather than putting it off until the next one.

While she waited for the plow to turn on State Route 74, Jamie lifted one gloved hand from the steering wheel and flexed it and then the other. She pressed the accelerator to follow the plow. Her car stalled. She turned the key to restart it. The engine made a feeble vroom and stopped. Jamie pressed the button for her hazard light. The signal on the dashboard didn't flash.

Certain the battery must be dead, she got out, opened the hood and checked the terminal connections. They were tight. She had jumper cables in the back. Maybe she could flag down the next car to come along and get a jump. *Or maybe not.* The alternator belt was missing. It must have broken and fallen off between here and the house.

She left the hood up and climbed back in the vehicle to call for a tow truck. Her old van had been in and out of the shop for service so many times last year that she had the number memorized.

"Hill's Auto Repair."

"Tom, it's Jamie Glasser. I'm stuck at the end of my road."

"Are you okay? Are you off the road? This storm is looking to be a real beast."

"I'm fine. The car's on the road. It stalled out. Looks like the alternator belt broke and the battery's dead."

"It may be a while. Jack has the truck out on another tow. I hate to make you sit there and wait. If the Longs are home, their boys could push your car into their driveway and give you a ride home."

"That would work, except that I was on my way to pick up Rose and Opal from Scouts."

"Don't worry. I'll call Eli. He was just here taking care of his mother's repair bill. He'll be going right by there."

"You don't have to do that." A red pickup turned the corner and stopped parallel to her. "He's already here."

Eli knocked on the window and she opened the door a crack so he could hear her. "I can't open the window. The car's dead."

He stepped back. "I can take a look at it. I have tools in the truck."

"Thanks. But there's nothing you can do." She explained the situation.

Eli opened the door the rest of the way. "You must be cold. Get in the truck. I have a tow chain. I'll pull your car into the Longs' driveway. You can run up to the house and let them know it's there, and we'll pick up Opal and Rose."

He offered his arm to help her across the slick pavement. She linked her arm around his elbow, feeling his strength beneath her hand. It had been a long time since she'd accepted anyone's support.

He opened the door. "Watch your step."

Jamie climbed in and settled into the heated

leather seat. She hadn't realized how cold she was until the heat of the cab hit her.

He joined her in the cab and pulled the truck across the road into the Longs' driveway to turn around so that he could hook up her vehicle for the tow.

"While I get your car, see if one or both of the boys are around to help me push it into the turnaround so it's not blocking the driveway."

"I can help you."

"I know, but why should you if we have free teenage labor to do it?"

She laughed. "Good point."

Jamie and both of the Long boys were waiting in the turnaround when Eli got back. While she was up at the house, she'd tried to call the scout leader with no success. She'd had service on the road, but five hundred feet away at the house her cell phone had no service bars. And the Longs' cable phone was out because of the storm.

Eli and the boys made quick work of detaching her vehicle and moving it into the turnaround so they could be back on their way.

"I tried to get Tom on the phone to let him know we moved the car, but I don't have any reception." He maneuvered the truck around and pulled onto the road.

"Me, neither. I just tried to call the girls' scout leader."

"Where are we going?" he asked.

"The school." She checked the clock on the dash-board. "I wish I could have gotten through. I was supposed to have been there to pick them up a half hour ago."

"Hey, you tried. You would have been early if you hadn't had car trouble. And you can't be the only parent delayed by the storm."

She formed a steeple with her hands and pressed her fingertips to her lips. His ready encouragement gave her a glimpse of how Eli dealt with the kids as a guidance counselor and youth group leader. "I don't want to wish anyone harm. But I wouldn't mind if some of the others were late."

She dropped her hands to her lap. Especially after last Saturday when the leader couldn't get through to her about the early finish to the Fort Ticonderoga trip and Charlotte had brought Rose and Opal home.

Jamie studied Eli's profile out of the corner of her eye. The aquiline nose, strong cheekbones. Char-lotte's oldest son, Brett, flashed in her mind. The college student had the same sandy brown hair as Eli. Did he have his other features, too?

"Don't worry. I'll get you there to pick up Rose and Opal."

"Hmm?"

"Your expression. You looked concerned."

"Not about that." She pressed her lips together.

"Myles told me something when he came home today. About something that happened at school."

"He didn't come in and talk with me about anything."

"He wouldn't have."

Eli straightened and leaned back in the seat.

"Some of the kids…" She clasped her hands in her lap. "Liam Russell was taunting him about you and me."

"That woman!" He stopped. "I take it Myles didn't like the idea."

"No. I set him straight that nothing is going on between us."

He stared ahead, seemingly intent on his driving. "Good."

His sharp tone slashed through the small distance separating them. She looked down at her hands. "Can I ask you a question?"

"Shoot."

"You and Charlotte."

His jaw tightened.

"Is…" She swallowed. "Is Brett yours?"

"No." The single word reverberated off the close walls of the truck cab.

Jamie shifted over toward the door. "That's what Liam told Myles."

"And that I refused to acknowledge him," Eli finished for her. "Brett isn't mine. Couldn't be mine. Charlie wanted to use me as her ticket out of Paradox Lake. I don't know, or care, what she thinks now."

"I told Myles not to repeat things he didn't know were true."

"Answer a question for me. Did you think it was true?"

She shrank down in the seat. A part of her had wondered. "I didn't think you would do that. Or that your mother would have let you if you'd tried."

He released a humorless laugh. "You're assigning my mother a whole lot more control over me than she had then."

"It's none of my business. I only wanted to let you know there was talk at school."

"No, I want to get what everyone else in Paradox Lake already knows out front and center for you. When I came home on leave after basic training, Charlie was pregnant. We'd gone out a couple of times. Nothing serious on my part. Or on hers."

"You don't have to explain."

"Yes." His voice softened, sending a pulse radiating down her spine. "Yes, I do. When I denied Charlie's accusations, my mother wanted me to take a paternity test. I told her that my word should be enough and that she and everyone else could believe whatever they wanted to believe."

Jamie reached over and touched his arm. "She was trying to protect you."

"Yeah, I realized that later, much later. While I

was somewhat of a troublemaker, I didn't lie to my mother—not about anything important. She should have known that."

Jamie pictured a seventeen-year-old Eli, back from basic training, full of himself and earnest in his righteousness. "For what it's worth, I believe you."

"It's worth a lot. A whole lot."

Eli turned into the snowy school parking lot. The impact of Jamie's statement and the force of his reply had surprised him. He looked at his office window and grimaced. He'd better put a stop to any lingering gossip at school tomorrow. It wasn't good for Charlie's kids, Myles or him. Across the parking lot, two cars sat parked near the school door, one snow covered and one fairly clean. "See, someone else is late, too." His voice boomed in the quiet cab.

Jamie smiled. "I'll only be a couple of minutes."

He watched her cross in front of the truck and, head down against the wind, make her way up the sidewalk toward the school. Right before she reached the steps, her feet flew out from beneath her and she landed flat on her back on the walk. Eli's heart stopped. He threw open the truck door and raced over.

"Are you all right?"

She propped herself up on one elbow and rubbed the back of her head. "I think so."

He offered his one hand and slipped the other under her elbow as she rose. They stood completely still, him looking down at her upturned face into the depths of her coffee-brown eyes. He tilted his head and leaned closer.

"Seriously." Charlie Russell stood at the top of the steps behind Jamie.

Jamie spun around to face her. "I slipped on the ice."

He squeezed her elbow. She didn't have to explain herself, them, to anyone, especially not Charlie.

"Well, sure." Charlie's gaze flitted between him and Jamie as she dragged her daughter down the stairs. "Rose and Opal are the last ones left."

"We'd better go in, then." Jamie looked back and gave him a heart-stopping smile—or what would have been a heart-stopping smile if it had reached her eyes and hadn't had an icy quality that rivaled the snow pelting them.

But, by the way Charlie huffed on her way to her car, all she had caught was the smile.

She marched up the stairs, shoulders back, eyes straight ahead with a precision that would have done a drill instructor proud.

"Jamie, you're here," the scout leader said as they entered the school cafeteria. "When you didn't call, I was worried you'd had car trouble..." Her gaze moved past Jamie to Eli. "Or something."

Jamie stiffened. "I did have car trouble and

couldn't get a cell connection. Eli came along and gave me a lift." She turned slightly toward him. "Have you met Eli Payton?"

"No, but I've heard of him."

Eli bristled. What was that supposed to mean? He was standing right here. He looked at the scout leader hard and she started.

"Of course," Jamie said. "At the high school back-to-school night, but you didn't get to meet him?"

The scout leader hadn't been at back-to-school night. There were few enough parents there that he'd remember seeing her. And from the satisfied expression on Jamie's face, she knew the leader hadn't been at back-to-school night. This was a side of Jamie that he'd only suspected before. He made a mental note to himself to avoid ever being on the strike side of her barbs.

"Where are my manners? Eli, this is Sonja Hephlin. Sonja, Eli Payton."

They nodded to each other.

"Come on, girls. Let's go." Jamie put an arm around each of the girls. "See you next week," she threw over her shoulder to Sonja and walked away.

"Nice to meet you," Eli said, unable to escape his upbringing and years of training in personnel.

"Same here." Her sour expression belied her words and made him wonder what Charlie had said to her. Not that it mattered to him. But it might to Jamie, especially if Rose and Opal had overheard.

He caught up with Jamie and the girls and opened the cab doors for them.

Jamie slumped in the seat beside him.

"You okay?"

"Fine, although I'll probably have a doozy of a bruise tomorrow."

He hadn't meant her fall. He should let it drop. She wasn't one of his students who needed him to draw out her problems and concerns. "I'll take care of Charlie."

"Who's Charlie?" Opal piped up.

He winced. He'd forgotten about the little ears in the backseat.

"I think he means Katy's mother," Rose answered.

"Is she hurt or something? She looked okay to me, except kind of mad when she was talking to Ms. Hephlin."

Fatigue shadowed on Jamie's porcelain-like face. "Opal, it's not nice to talk about other people."

Which was only one of the reasons he was going to take care of Charlie whether Jamie wanted him to or not.

Aside from the girls fidgeting in the back, they rode the rest of the way to Jamie's house in silence.

He pulled into the empty driveway. "Do you need to get into work tomorrow?"

"No, I'm not scheduled in the office and Kelly or

Autumn can swing by and pick me up if we have a birth."

"If you do need a car, call. I'm sure you could borrow Mom's. She's holed up in her studio working on a new project and probably wouldn't even notice if it were gone."

"Thanks. I'll call her if I do. But, hopefully, Tom will have mine fixed tomorrow." She turned toward the backseat. "You guys go in. I want to talk with Mr. Payton for a minute."

Eli looked out the side window at the wind whipping the trees lining Jamie's yard.

"Grown-up stuff. Boring." Opal scrunched her face and Rose rolled her eyes. "Bye, Mr. Payton." They waved back at him as they trudged through the heavy snow.

"You should get Myles out here to shovel the walk and driveway or no one will be able to get in tomorrow, if you need to go out."

She frowned. "We'll take care of it."

Why couldn't he keep his mouth shut? He fiddled with the truck keys.

She cleared her throat. "I appreciate your offering to run interference for me with Charlotte. But please don't."

He bit the side of his mouth to stop himself from blurting out, "Why not?"

"Obviously she's spreading gossip about you and me." She eyed him. "For whatever reason."

Eli slapped the keys against his thigh. It stung that she might think he'd done anything to intentionally cause Charlie's viciousness. For the first time in years he thought about having the paternity test his mother had pushed when Charlie had made her initial accusations. Eli had been sober enough that night he and Charlie had spent at the Maple Shade Motel to know nothing had happened. But he'd begrudgingly give Charlie the benefit of the doubt that maybe she hadn't been. If the test would shut the woman up, it might be worth doing.

"I don't know if I can stay out of it."

A muscle in Jamie's cheek worked as if forming her next words.

No! He palmed his thigh. This wasn't about him and old grudges. It was about Jamie. Charlie's stories hurt Jamie a lot more than him. "What do you want me to do?"

She leaned toward him. "We need to avoid being seen together. If we don't give Charlotte anything to talk about, she won't have anything to say about us."

He doubted that. But Jamie looked so serious. Too serious.

"Ah." He controlled the grin tugging at his lips. "So we should sneak around so no one sees us."

Her eyes went blank. Then, a blush rose on her cheeks, kicking his protective instincts into full force. Jamie was an intriguing puzzle of independence and vulnerability.

"No!" She laughed and raised her hand as if to swat him, then dropped it. "I like being with you."

He pressed his shoulders back into the seat.

"As a friend," she finished. "But Charlotte's gossip isn't good for the kids." Her voice dropped. "Or for me. Rose doesn't understand why Katy can't come over anymore. And Myles is angry and hurt. He thinks I...we're betraying his father somehow."

"Myles is a teenage boy who's trying to be the man of the house. He'd think that about any man you were seeing."

"But I'm not seeing you."

That sliced his ego in half. "So, what, we avoid each other?"

She released a sigh, making him feel like a petulant child. "We limit our contact to a guidance counselor/parent relationship."

"I can do that." But he wasn't going to like it. "So, I'll look for an opening in one of the other bowling leagues."

"Of course not. I'm the newbie. I'll drop out."

"Come on. You don't want to do that."

She scrunched her face in an expression that was a mirror image of Opal's earlier one. He waited for her argument.

"You're right. I don't want to quit." She grinned. "At least not before I beat you. We'll set some rules."

He took that to mean she'd set some rules.

"You don't walk me to my car. No buying me

the cheeseburger special. Nothing that would lead anyone to think we're anything but teammates. Because we're not."

He got it. She'd already hit the strike zone with that pitch.

The curtain at the living room window moved. "Don't look now, but we're being watched," he said.

"Add no sitting in the car and talking to the list." She made an invisible check in the air. "Seriously, I should be going in."

Eli reached for his door handle.

"You don't need to walk me in."

He got out of the truck and walked around to open her door. "I'll wait until you get to the door."

Her lips parted and snapped shut as if she were going to tell him that wasn't necessary, either, but decided not to.

She climbed out. "Thanks. For everything. I'm sure you had better things you could have been doing."

"No problem." He stood by the truck watching Jamie walk to the house, head down against the wind. She waved as she closed the front door behind her.

Right now, he couldn't think of anything he'd rather have been doing than spending time with Jamie—except spending time with Jamie *and* protecting her from Charlie Russell. But he'd promised

Jamie he wouldn't step in between her and Charlie unless it was on Jamie's terms. Terms that weren't going to be easy to honor.

Chapter Nine

"Eli. Brett Russell is here to see you. Are you available?"

While it wasn't like her to make a mistake, Thelma Woods, the school office manager, must have meant Liam—Brett had graduated last year. Eli eyed the reports piled up on his desk. "Yes, send him down." His job was to counsel students, not push paper.

The door opened slowly and the young man entered the office.

Eli snapped the pencil he was holding. He couldn't believe Charlie would stoop this low, using her own child.

"Mr. Payton, I'm Brett Russell." He offered his hand.

Eli rose, letting the pencil piece in his hand fall to the desk, and walked around the desk to shake Brett's hand. "Have a seat." Eli motioned to the chair next to his desk and returned to his seat. "What can I do for you?"

Brett kept his gaze lowered. "My mother…"

Eli tensed.

"She says that she's going to hit you with a paternity suit to pay for my college."

"She sent you here to tell me that?"

Brett's head shot up. "No! She doesn't know I'm here. I came to ask you a favor."

The kid was as brash as his mother.

Brett shook his head. "I have no right to ask anything of you after my mother's behavior toward you."

"I'm not your father." Might as well get that right out front.

"I know you're not my father. Dad told me the whole story a long time ago. They were arguing in their room and I overheard Mom taunt Dad that he wasn't my father. When Dad came out, I was still in the hall. Mom's a very unhappy person. She's gone kind of crazy since Dad left, talking about the past a lot and what she could have done, how she wouldn't be working at a hardware store in a Podunk town if you hadn't left her. I think she's convinced herself that you *are* my father and owe her for ruining her life."

Eli's compassion for Brett clashed with his anger at Charlie. His anger won. "She's not going to collect on that. She's hurt a lot of people." *People I care about.*

"I'm sorry. She's so mad at Dad. She says she's not taking anything from him and I shouldn't, either. He's been paying for my classes at North Country Community College and helping with my apartment in Ticonderoga."

"I don't follow." An edge crept into his voice. "What does any of this have to do with me, except in your mother's mind?"

Brett studied his fingers. "Nothing. I'm messing this up. Mom thinks she can force you to send me away to college. I'm so tired of hearing her rants about you and how you owe her big-time and about how none of her kids are going to get stuck in Paradox Lake."

Eli softened. The same way he was tired of hearing Charlie's lies spread all over town.

"I've come up with an idea that might stop her."

Eli frowned. He'd promised Jamie not to interfere, to let the gossip die of its own accord. But he had a personal stake in Charlie's actions, too.

"I wouldn't blame you if you asked me to leave right now, but hear me out."

"All right."

"Mom keeps giving me all these college catalogs. When I graduated last year, I wasn't even sure I wanted to go to college. I had good grades and all, but I didn't know what I wanted to study. I thought about joining the service. She talked me out of that and compromised with my taking classes at the community college this year."

Eli interrupted. "I'm certainly not the person to change your mother's mind, if that's what you're getting to."

"No, I doubt all four branches of the Armed Forces combined could do that."

Eli laughed. He couldn't help himself.

"I started looking at the service academies. I know most kids apply to start right out of high school. But online, it says the Air Force academy can accept students up to age twenty-three."

"The academy is a better way to go than the route I took."

"That's kind of what my favor is about."

"I don't think I can help you."

Brett's face crumpled.

"I'm just a retired Lt. Colonel. I don't have the clout to recommend your appointment."

"I know. I need to contact our U.S. representative and senator." Brett scuffed his boot on the floor. "My friend Seth says you're a good guy, that you'd help me prep to apply. There's this whole list of things online."

Eli studied the young man across from him. He had a lot of nerve after what Charlie had put Eli and his mother and now Jamie, through. But he was a kid. He probably didn't know half of what his mother had done.

A verse from his Bible in a Year online study group played in his mind: *Do not judge, and you will not be judged. Do not condemn, and you will not be condemned. Forgive and you will be forgiven.*

"It could get my mother off my back and yours. You know, get her to drop the whole lawsuit thing."

Eli couldn't ignore the plea in Brett's eyes. Brett wasn't responsible for his mother's actions. It was up to God, not Eli, to judge and punish if punishment was needed. "Yes, I'll do what I can."

"Thanks, sir."

Eli wondered whether the kid was brown-nosing him with the *sir*. It didn't matter. "I'm free after church on Sunday to get together."

"What time would that be?"

"One is good. We can meet at the North Country library. You have computer access there, right?"

Brett nodded.

"Fine."

Brett stood as if to leave but didn't move.

"Is there something else?"

The young man's gaze dropped. "I…my mother… never mind. Thanks again."

"You're welcome."

He turned and left.

As Eli had thought before, Brett had a lot of chutzpah to come here and ask a favor. But now that he'd talked with Brett, he could separate Brett from Charlie. And the kid's plan just might work. That and another idea he had, if Brett would agree. Eli took a new pencil from the desk drawer and tapped it on the desk. He wouldn't be going against his promise to Jamie. Not really.

Jamie's heart pounded as she approached Hazard-town Community Church.

"Watch it, Mom!" Myles said.

She braked just in time to miss the deer dashing across the highway in front of her. The pounding doubled.

Dear Lord— She cut the involuntary prayer short.

"That was a close one."

"You've got that right. Thanks, I didn't see it." What was wrong with her? She'd lived in the North Country long enough to be on alert for deer darting into the road. Driving Myles to his first confirmation class shouldn't have her so rattled. She shuddered thinking what could have happened if she'd hit the deer. She had all of the kids with her.

Jamie parked at the back of the church lot, since she wouldn't be staying. She scanned the sparsely filled lot for Eli's truck before getting out. She couldn't help it. She hadn't seen him for a couple of weeks. Rose had come down with some kind of bug the Friday before last, and Jamie hadn't made bowling. Eli never showed this past Friday. She should be glad he was honoring her request to limit their contact. But she missed him. Missed his strength, his smile and even his take-charge manner that bordered on bossiness.

The click of Myles's door opening pulled her from her thoughts. "You need to come in and sign me up. Pastor Joel said so when I talked to him at youth group."

"I know." She got out and opened the back door for Rose and Opal.

"Can I go say hi to my Sunday school teacher?" Opal asked as they entered the church hall. *Former Sunday school teacher,* Jamie silently corrected her daughter. "No, stay with me. We're early. She's probably not here yet."

Opal pushed out her lower lip and followed Jamie to the room where Myles's class was. Jamie hated saying no. Opal had adored her teacher and hadn't seen her since they'd left Community Church. But she knew Opal would want to stay for class. And she wasn't up to that confrontation. She'd had her reasons for the break, and they hadn't changed.

She looked at Myles. He was older, old enough to choose for himself. Rose and Opal could have that choice later when their choice wouldn't drag Jamie back into participating at church.

"Myles, Jamie. Good to see you." Pastor Joel met them at the classroom door. "And Opal and Rose. Are you staying for Sunday school?"

Jamie's heart sank. She should have expected this. She'd explained to Rose and Opal why they weren't going to Sunday school anymore. That it was all a lie. But they were only five and seven when John died, and she'd been emotionally distraught. Who knew what they had gotten out of the explanation. She'd put them off when they'd asked again until they'd stopped asking to go.

"No, Mom won't let us. Only Myles," Rose said.

She liked Joel. But he wasn't playing fair. She was the parent. It was her decision whether or not they attended Sunday school. Her shoulders drooped. And it was Joel's job to gather his flock.

"I'm sorry," Pastor Joel apologized. "I assumed, or I should say, hoped."

"That's okay. Myles said you need me to sign something." Maybe she could get the girls back out to the car before they ran into anyone else.

"Yes." Pastor motioned her to the front of the room. "I'm asking all of the parents to sign a pledge that they will support their child in his or her decision to explore church membership."

Jamie read through the pledge. It seemed innocuous enough. She supported Myles learning more in hopes of helping him see the folly of blind faith and save him from the heartache she'd experienced. She wouldn't be lying by signing it. An abyss opened in her chest that stretched to the pit of her stomach.

She pressed the pen to the paper so hard she almost tore it and scratched her signature.

"The class is done at ten fifteen?"

"That's the plan."

"I'll be back then. Meet me outside, Myles." Everyone would be arriving for service then. The fewer people she ran into here, the better for the tenuous inner peace she'd built over the time since John's death.

Pastor Joel walked with her to the door, greeting the other arriving students. "You're sure you don't want to stay for Sunday school?" the pastor asked.

Opal and Rose looked at her with expectant eyes.

"You know a lot of the adult class members, Ted and Mary Hazard, Neal and Anne, Drew and Emily, the Hills, Becca Norton, Edna Tiffany, Harry Stowe and Leah Summers." Pastor Joel ran through the rest of the names like he was doing class roll call. "Leah's son, Eli, is leading the class now. Harry thought it was time to give someone else the opportunity."

Pastor Joel's mention of Eli tugged at her. He'd probably be a dynamic class leader. She pictured him, his wide shoulders and broad chest filling out a crisp dress shirt tucked neatly into sharply creased slacks. Jamie shook the picture out of her head. She couldn't believe she'd actually been considering attending the class just to watch Eli.

Pastor Joel misinterpreted her headshake. "I had to try. When you're ready, we'll welcome you back."

Her throat clogged. She'd yet to find something to fill the void that leaving Community Church had created. But she couldn't live a lie of pretended faith.

She touched Pastor Joel's arm. "That means a lot to me. But I can't. Come on, girls. Let's go."

Rose and Opal dallied walking back to the church hall, probably in hopes of seeing some of their Sunday school friends. Jamie fought the almost suffocating longing that had plagued her since she'd set foot in the church building. She stopped at the door to the hall and waited for the girls who were now several paces behind her whispering to each other.

"I can't explain it," Rose said in exasperation. "Ask Mom."

"Ask me what?"

"Rose said that Katy told her at school that Mr. Payton is Brett's father."

Jamie glanced up and down the hall. When she saw they were alone, she breathed a sigh of relief that did nothing to slow her racing heartbeat.

"How can that be? Brett already has a father. Or is Mr. Payton going to marry Katy's mother now that her father doesn't live with them anymore and be Brett's stepfather? I hope not because then Mr. Payton couldn't take me to the dinner-dance at school. And if he were Brett's stepfather, wouldn't he be Katy's stepfather, too?"

"This isn't the place to have this conversation. We'll talk about it later."

Opal grimaced. "Okay, I guess. I just don't get it."

Jamie herded the girls to the side door where they'd be less likely to run into anyone. Leaning against the bar to open the door, she almost lost her balance when her push met no resistance.

"Excuse me. Jamie!" Eli's mother, Leah, stood in the open doorway.

Jamie placed her hand over her heart. "Hi. You startled me. I didn't expect anyone to be coming in this door." She glanced over Leah's shoulder.

"Looking for Eli?" Leah tilted her head back and to the side where Jamie had glanced before stepping inside and closing the door behind her.

Yes, so I can avoid him. Her cheeks heated. "We missed him at bowling on Friday. I hope he hasn't come down with that bug that's going around. Rose was sick week before last."

"Oh, no, he's fine. Last weekend was his Air Guard weekend. He's probably in the classroom setting up for adult Sunday school."

"I didn't see his truck in the parking lot," Jamie said, digesting what Leah had told her. Eli was in the National Guard? He hadn't mentioned that to her. But why would he have? She swallowed hard. That meant he could be called up. Neal Hazard had served a year in Afghanistan with his Army Guard unit. All the more reason to keep some distance between her and Eli.

"It's at the parsonage," Leah said. "Pastor Joel

bought firewood, and it was a lot cheaper if he didn't have to pay to have it delivered. Eli volunteered to pick it up and some of the kids are going to unload it for Pastor Joel after confirmation class." Leah tilted her head toward the door Jamie had been trying to exit. "I take it you're not joining us this morning. Or were you running out to the car for something?" Leah added with a hopeful uplift to her voice.

This was why she wanted to run into as few people as possible at church this morning. Too many memories of good times spent with friends warring with bitter betrayal and loss. "No, I drove Myles over for the confirmation class. He wanted to take it, and I thought he was old enough to make that decision."

"Oh. I have to put these cookies for coffee hour in the kitchen and get to class. But before I do, I want to thank you."

"Thank me? For what?"

"For convincing Eli to do something I've wanted him to do for years."

Jamie had no idea what the other woman was talking about.

"He's taken a paternity test to stop Charlotte Russell from suing him for whatever she has in her head these days that she can sue him for concerning Brett. That poor boy."

Opal's question ran through Jamie's mind and her

heart sank. Eli had promised to let things die out on their own. The test would put a definitive end to speculation about Eli being Brett's father. But Jamie had a bad feeling that having the test now, after refusing to for all those years, would only antagonize Charlotte and, if she thought Eli was doing it for Jamie, possibly cause the woman to lash out against her and her family again.

"I didn't have anything to do with Eli's decision. In fact, I asked…" Jamie shook her head. She was being selfish, thinking of herself. It was Eli's decision. "Never mind. You want to get to class."

"Yes, I won't ever hear the end of it from Eli if I'm the last one there. Maybe we'll see you next week. The confirmation class is meeting for the next couple of months, right?"

"Through the middle of March." Jamie sidestepped Leah's invitation to the adult Sunday school class.

"I'll tell Eli you were asking about him."

Jamie mumbled something about getting the girls home, although now they'd spent so much time here that once she got home she'd almost have to turn right around to come back and pick up Myles.

She pushed the door open again and welcomed the chill of the day on her heated skin. She knew she shouldn't have come to church. It only caused her heartache.

When Jamie returned an hour later to pick up

Myles, he was nowhere to be seen. "I told him to meet me outside."

"Do you want me to go in and get him?" Rose offered.

Jamie had been talking to herself, not thinking about the girls in the back.

"I'll go, too," Opal piped up.

Jamie weighed letting them. When had she become such a coward? "We'll give him five minutes and if he doesn't come out, we'll all go in." *No matter how many people we may see and how many of them might ask me if we're going to service.*

Eli approached the driver's side of Jamie's vehicle. She rolled down the window and frowned at him. "Looking for Myles?" he asked.

"Yes, he was supposed to meet me by the church hall door."

"You weren't here yet when his class let out."

Her frown deepened.

"I couldn't have been more than a couple of minutes late."

He weighed whether to say he hadn't meant that as a criticism. He was glad she was late. But he had a feeling that saying so would get him deeper into whatever quicksand he was already sinking into.

"Myles went over to the parsonage with Drew and a couple of the other guys from the youth group to unload Pastor Joel's firewood. I told Pastor I'd be on the lookout for you and let you know where Myles was." At the time, it had seemed like a good way to see Jamie and talk with her without violating any of their agreed-upon rules.

"Fine. Thanks. I'll drive over and get him."

"Mind if I tag along and pick up my truck? I lent it to Pastor Joel. Getting it now would save me some time. After service, I want to pick up a sub at the General Store and be home in time for kick-off." Hoping to garner a smile from Jamie, he teased her. "The Buffalo game is on since the Giants have a bye week. Not that I'll be watching that game." The smile didn't materialize.

"No, I…"

He stilled. Obviously, she wasn't in a teasing mood. But what he'd said didn't warrant not giving him a lift.

"I don't mind."

Or, from her tone, she didn't mind so much that she'd say no. He crossed in front of her vehicle to the passenger side.

"Eli."

He looked across the parking lot to see his mother waving at him from the church hall doorway.

She hurried across the pavement. "We need some help rearranging the table for coffee hour after service."

"Jamie was going to give me a lift over to Pastor Joel's house so I won't have to walk over later." Of course, any number of other people, including Mom, could, and would, give him a lift. But he hadn't seen Jamie since the evening her car had broken down and he'd reluctantly agreed they should avoid each other for a while. He'd missed her more than he'd thought he would.

"Oh, sure, you go ahead. I can find someone else."

He reached for the door handle.

"Wait." She motioned to Jamie to open the passenger side window so she could hear her and stepped over to vehicle. "Since you're not going to service…" His mother paused. "Unless you've changed your mind?"

"No, I haven't."

"Then why don't I take the girls in to get some cookies to take home with them while you drive Eli over to get his truck? I made more than enough cookies that a few of them won't be missed."

His mother wasn't being very subtle, either in her desire to have Jamie attend service or in her matchmaking.

"Can we, Mom?" Rose and Opal asked in unison.

He waited for Jamie to come up with an excuse as to why they couldn't.

"Yes, I guess it would be all right."

Eli hadn't expected her to give up the buffer between them that having the girls in the backseat provided. Maybe she'd missed him, too.

Opal and Rose tumbled from the vehicle.

"You stay with Ms. Summers."

"We will."

"I'll send Myles in to get you when I come back."

Eli opened the door and climbed in. His knees were almost touching the dashboard. "Mind if I move the seat back?"

"No, go ahead."

He felt her gaze on him as he adjusted the seat. When he'd finished, she put the vehicle in gear and pulled out of the parking lot.

"I let the girls go with your mother so we could have a couple of minutes to talk."

He settled into the seat with satisfaction. *She had missed him, too.*

"Your mother told me."

His mother could have told her any number of things, but the edge to Jamie's voice told him that what Mom had said wasn't something good.

"About the paternity test. She thanked me for encouraging you to do it. Except, as you know, I didn't. I'm trying to distance myself from anything to do with Charlotte and you."

Eli swallowed hard. When he'd told his mother, it hadn't occurred to him that she would share the information, especially with Jamie.

"Why now?" she asked.

Before he could answer, she put her hand up, palm

out. "No, I don't need to know. I understand having this dredged up is difficult for you. But you need to realize and consider what Charlie is doing to my family. Rose can't see her best friend, except at school. Myles is getting in fights. And Opal is asking me questions a seven-year-old shouldn't be asking."

Her cell phone chimed, halting her torrent of words.

"I have to check this. It could be the birthing center." She pulled over to the shoulder of the road and tapped her phone. Her face paled. "And now this." She shoved the phone at him, and he listened to the message.

"This is a warning. For your own good, stay away from Eli Payton. He's not the wonder boy everyone in Paradox Lake seems to think he is. He'll leave you behind, just like he left me behind, like your husband left you."

Eli squeezed the phone so hard he feared he'd break it. Charlie had gone way too far. He dropped the phone into the console between them and instinctively reached for Jamie. She leaned forward almost into his arms before jerking back. Wiping her eye, she shook her head.

His chest tightened with helplessness. "I'm having the test done to put an end to Charlie's machinations once and for all. Everything will be fine if things go as planned."

"As who planned?"

He could mention the conversation with Brett, but, when they'd met at the library, he'd given his word to the teen that he wouldn't tell anyone what they were doing. Not yet. "Trust me. I have everything under control."

"Trust you." Her voice dropped to a whisper, as if she were talking to herself. "Like I trusted John when he always said he'd come home safe and when he'd said his tour in Afghanistan would be his last. I found out after that he'd reenlisted without telling me. I trusted God to watch over all of us. See where that got me?"

She finished with a dry bark of a laugh that ripped through Eli's insides. He wasn't John. "My word is good. I always take care of my unfinished business."

Jamie blinked and tapped her gloved finger on the steering wheel. "You do that. Just make sure my kids aren't collateral damage." She pressed her lips together and lifted her chin, ready to confront the world one on one.

His heart twisted. But she didn't have to do it all alone. She could let others help her. She could let him help her.

As they rode in silence to Pastor Joel's, Eli gave up a prayer for help in doing right by Jamie and for her to realize that God hadn't forsaken her. She just had to open her heart again to Him.

"Where's your truck?" she asked, as the house came in sight.

"Out back. The guys are stacking the wood on the deck."

She pulled to the end of the driveway, and he opened the door. "I'll tell Myles you're here."

"Thanks."

Eli strode over to Myles. "Your mother is here to pick you up."

Myles glared at him. The teen had avoided all contact at school and youth group since Liam had embarrassed him at school.

"She gave me a lift over from church."

Myles's glare intensified.

Swift. It hadn't been necessary to tell Myles that Jamie had driven him over. Just being with Jamie for a few minutes had upset his equilibrium and reduced Eli to the level of one of his students attempting to establish male authority with another.

The teen added another log to the stack.

"She's waiting." Myles could dislike him all he wanted, but Eli wouldn't stand for him disrespecting Jamie.

Myles tossed the log in his hand toward the pile and stalked off.

"Hey, Eli." Drew Stacey waved him over to

where he stood on the driveway side of Eli's emptied truck. "So, what's up?" Drew tipped his head toward Jamie's departing vehicle.

"Nothing." Unfortunately. "Nothing at all."

Chapter Ten

"Becca, come on back. Autumn will be with us in a couple of minutes." Jamie led the expectant mother to the examination room for her Tuesday morning appointment. "How have you been?"

"Not bad, but I'm hitting that tired-all-the-time stage. What I wouldn't give to trade my afternoon economics class for a nap."

Jamie laughed. "I can remember that. Step on the scale."

Becca grimaced and obliged.

Jamie recorded the figure on her iPad and they walked to the exam room. Becca sat on the examination table and Jamie took her blood pressure. "Looks fine. Any questions while we wait for Autumn?"

"Yes, but not about the baby. I'm chairing Career Day at school."

"As if you don't have enough to do."

Becca laughed. "I guess you would know, and that's why I hesitate to ask."

"Uh-oh. Do I want to hear this?"

"Sure you do. It's for the kids."

Jamie groaned. "My weak spot."

"That's what I'm hoping. Could I talk you into putting together a booth for the Adirondack Medical Center?"

Jamie pressed her forefinger to her lips. While she was flattered, Becca was right. She didn't have a lot of spare time. "You mean the birthing center."

"No." Becca gently swung her feet back and forth. "The Medical Center. With the birthing center, clinics and the hospital in Saranac Lake, it's one of the area's largest employers."

"Wouldn't you rather have Kelly or Autumn or one of the administrators represent the Adirondack Medical Center? Autumn's a hometown girl."

Becca glanced at the door. "I thought about Autumn. But you have more work experience, and..." She dropped her gaze to her hands folded in her lap. "Your experience is more in the trenches, if you know what I mean."

"Not exactly."

Becca leaned forward. "A fair number of our students' parents aren't college-educated, and we have students who are planning to go to work right out of high school."

Excitement bubbled through Jamie. "Like licensed practical nurses or aides or lab techs or food service." Jamie could relate to that. She'd taken LPN courses at Vo-Tech when she was in high school and worked as an LPN until John was deployed to the Middle East the first time. Then, she decided to go to college and become an RN.

"Exactly." Becca slapped the examination table. "As I said, someone who came up through the trenches. I think you can put together a great booth that will really give the kids direction. And I certainly have nothing against you asking Autumn to help."

The door to the examination room pushed open. "Asking Autumn to help with what?" the midwife asked.

"Jamie's going to…I mean, Jamie is thinking about heading up a booth for the medical center at the high school Career Day."

"Good choice and, sure, I'll help," Autumn said.

"Why do I feel I have no choice?" Jamie asked her friends with a surrendering smile.

"Because you want to," Becca said.

Jamie thought about the conflicted feelings she'd had last Sunday when she'd dropped Myles off for his class. The longing for the fellowship she'd once had there. Career Day would be a non-church way for her to get involved in the community again.

"Yes, because I want to."

Becca clapped. "Now, I almost have all the booths set."

"Of course," Jamie warned, "if Autumn and I have a birth on Career Day, our booth might be unmanned."

"Not a problem. I'm sure you'll have it set up so well it can run on its own. Our first meeting is Friday evening in my homeroom. The school will be open for the basketball game anyway. Can you make it?"

Friday was bowling. But after her and Eli's discussion on Sunday, she wasn't sure she was up to spending the evening with him.

"If you're concerned about Myles watching the girls, I can take them all to the game," Autumn offered. "I wouldn't mind. Myles could hang out with Tanner, and I enjoy spending time with Rose and Opal."

"Thanks. I'll be there."

Another week away from Eli would give her time to put him and the situation with Charlotte and her son back into perspective.

Jamie sat in the living room recliner basking in her few moments of solitude. Autumn had picked up the kids an hour ago so they could stop for pizza before the game. Scooby came over and nuzzled Jamie's foot. She rubbed his nose. "Yes, it is quiet with them all gone. Come on, I'll feed you. Then, I'm leaving, too." Scooby whimpered as if he understood.

With the dog fed, Jamie headed over to the school. She hadn't asked Becca who else was on the Career Day committee, but she'd find out soon enough. Both the stairwell and the hall to Becca's classroom were empty, even though, according to her watch, she was only fifteen minutes early. She could have sat and enjoyed her solitude at home a little longer. But as long as the classroom was open, she could sit and enjoy her solitude here.

The doorknob turned and, as she pushed the door open, her heart tripped. She took in the broad shoulders, perfect posture, the way his close-cropped hair tapered to a V on the back of his neck. Eli sat in the student desk directly in front of Becca's desk tapping something into his tablet computer. She pulled the door back toward her and it squeaked.

He turned. "Jamie. Becca said she'd talked you into joining us."

Funny, she hadn't said anything to Jamie about Eli being on the committee.

He glanced at his watch.

"Hi, Eli. Yes, I'm here fifteen minutes early."

"What?" Confusion spread across his face.

"You checked your watch. You do it often. Or often when I meet with you."

The laugh lines at the corners of his eyes deepened. "Bad habit. It's from a combination of my mother always being late and me serving in the military."

Jamie took her coat off and placed it on the desk behind her before sliding into the seat next to him. "I'm surprised Becca isn't here yet."

"Me, too." He moved his arm with his watch away from him on the desk as if to stop himself from checking it.

Jamie suppressed a smile. "Becca didn't mention anything to me about you being here tonight."

"I asked her not to. After last Sunday, I was afraid you'd turn her down."

The truth stung. She might have.

"Becca really wanted you to agree."

"It's fine. I'm kind of excited about putting together a booth for the Medical Center. And I should have known you'd be involved. You're the guidance counselor."

"I can help you get organized. I mean, I've done this sort of thing before. I spent some time on an Air Force recruitment team."

Jamie froze. Eli had been a recruiter. John had been recruited at a job fair. It hadn't been at their high school—it had been at a local mall—and Eli certainly hadn't been involved. Still, resentment squeezed her chest. If the recruiters hadn't been there, John would be... She pushed her thoughts back into the mental folder where she kept the remembrances of John and their marriage and clamped down on the feeling of betrayal she felt for her attraction to Eli. As irritating as he could be, she couldn't deny the pull between them. Not that she could see anything coming of it. She couldn't let herself care for another man the military could take away from her.

Eli couldn't miss the rigid way Jamie held herself. Apparently, he'd said something wrong yet again. He couldn't tell whether it was his offer to help her with her organization or his mention of recruiting.

"Hey, you two." Becca breezed into the classroom. "I meant to be here at six forty-five."

Eli caught Jamie's gaze darting from his face to his wrist and back. He grinned at her and she turned her attention to a folder she'd placed in front of her.

Becca set her briefcase on her desk and began removing papers. "My sitter cancelled this morning and I had to ask my former mother-in-law to watch Brendon. I couldn't escape a thinly veiled admonishment about how I should be home with him, shouldn't have taken on this committee if it meant evening meetings. But you don't want to hear my woes. Jamie, just let me say that I don't know how you do it with three kids."

"It's a challenge, but I manage. Usually."

And surprisingly well. Although Eli didn't know

why he was surprised. He was coming around to the realization that she was a lot better organized than he'd given her credit for at first, and competent at a surprising number of different things. Still, she could let a guy lend a hand every so often.

"So, did you two come together?" Becca put her emptied case on the floor beside her.

"No." Jamie drew the word out. "Why would you think that?"

"I thought you were dating." Becca's hands fluttered as she rearranged the papers she'd placed on her desk.

"Whatever gave you that idea?" Jamie asked.

"The other day after dismissal I looked out of my window and saw Myles and Liam Russell fighting. Some of the other kids broke it up and everyone got on his bus. I talked with Myles after class the next day. He seemed upset that his mother was seeing someone." Becca paused. "Not that you shouldn't be. I suggested he talk with Eli, and Myles made it sound like it was Eli you were seeing, and he wasn't happy about it. Then Mrs. Woods said what a cute couple you make...."

Jamie blanched.

"And tonight, my mother-in-law mentioned that you're bowling together in the Friday night league." Becca's voice trailed off again and she looked at Eli.

"It's true."

Jamie's eyes widened. She hadn't caught his humor.

"We're bowling with Tom and Karen Hill." He tapped the toe of his boot against the desk leg. "That's it." Except there was something more. He just hadn't quite figured out what. He needed Jamie for that, and she seemed to be doing her best to avoid him.

"Right," Jamie agreed. "I signed up for the winter-spring bowling season. I had no idea Eli bowled, and it was completely random that we ended up on the same team."

Eli leaned back in his seat. To his ears, the lady was protesting too much. And, unless he was reading the schooled expression on Becca's face wrong, she agreed.

"I guess that's settled," Becca said. "I'm expecting a few more people, speaking of whom." She lifted her chin toward the door.

Anne Howard Hazard, Jamie's former neighbor and a professor at the community college, Liz Young from the Chamber of Commerce and another woman Eli didn't recognize entered the room together.

"Come in. Take a seat, any seat." Becca waved them in. "I think you all know each other, except Tessa Hamilton. Tessa's taken over the movie theater. She's going to coordinate local business representation at Career Day and talk with some of the chain stores in Ticonderoga about participating."

"Hi," Tessa said. "I met Anne and Liz in the hall."

"This is Jamie Glasser. She's a labor and delivery nurse with a midwife practice at the Adirondack Medical Center birthing center in Ticonderoga. And the handsome gentleman next to her is our high school guidance counselor, Eli Payton."

Wrinkles creased Jamie's forehead. Eli could almost believe Becca's compliment had made Jamie jealous. Behind him, the classroom door clicked open and shut.

"Hey, sorry I'm late. Brett's car isn't running, so I had to pick him up at the college and give him a lift to his place. Of course, he didn't call until I had already driven home from Ticonderoga." Patrick Russell smiled and greeted Becca, Jamie and the other women. His smile disappeared when he got to Eli. "Payton."

Eli didn't miss Patrick's use of his last name, just like they'd done when they'd been rivals for the starting quarterback position on the Schroon Lake Central football team.

"Patrick."

"Why don't you take the seat on the other side of Eli?"

Patrick shrugged out of his overcoat and sat.

Silence hung in the air. Tessa glanced around at her fellow committee members as if trying to measure the situation.

"Sorry, Tessa," Becca said. "This is Patrick Russell. He's a sales manager with International

Paper in Ticonderoga, another one of the area's large employers."

"Nice to meet you."

"Hi, Tessa."

"Tessa inherited the Schroon Lake movie theater from her grandfather. Now that we have all of the introductions out of the way, let's get down to business. Here's an outline of what I've put together so far." Becca passed a copy to each of the committee members. "It gives you an idea of the businesses that will be represented. Any questions, additions?"

"I see you've included recruiters from the Armed Services," Jamie said, looking directly at Eli.

"Representatives, not recruiters," he corrected in an effort to deflect Jamie's opposition.

Jamie turned her attention back to the outline. He understood where she was coming from, probably better than she thought he did. But he thought her opposition was unfounded. The military was a career option students should know about. Personally, he wouldn't have been against allowing active recruitment of seniors who were old enough to sign up without parental permission. All of the branches required a high school diploma or equivalency now, so it wasn't like they'd be pulling students out of school. He'd enlisted at seventeen with his mother's permission and hadn't regretted it and, as far as he could tell, neither had Jamie's husband. He'd re-upped several times.

"We always have them." Becca backed up Eli. She glanced up and down the line of committee members sitting in front of her, ending with Jamie.

Everyone on the committee, save Tessa, knew Jamie's situation. Anne and Liz gave her sympathetic looks.

"Don't you remember from the years you were school nurse?" Becca asked.

"I guess I didn't notice then." Her voice was almost inaudible. "I don't suppose I could talk you out of it."

Becca bit her bottom lip and Eli waited for her to answer before he jumped in again. Becca was the committee chair, and he was sure Jamie already knew his answer.

"I'm sorry, but no," Becca said. "Our students need exposure to all available career options."

"That's what I thought."

Becca hesitated as if waiting to see if Jamie had more to say before asking, "Anyone else have comments, questions?"

"Not from me," Patrick said. "I was on the committee last year, too, with Liz and Anne."

"I may have some once I start putting together a list of local companies to contact," Tessa said. "Can I email you?"

"That would be fine. And I see you at school every day, Eli."

Eli couldn't resist a sidewise glance at Jamie to

see if she had any reaction to him and Becca seeing each other every day. She didn't, or was hiding it well. Maybe he'd imagined the spark of jealousy he'd seen on her face earlier.

"Okay." Becca lifted her phone from her case. "All we need to do is set a date for our next meeting. Let's make it in two weeks. That should give everyone time to get organized. What night?"

"Jamie and I bowl on Friday," Eli said, garnering a studied look from Patrick. "And Anne and I have Singles Plus on Thursdays," he added quickly to put the other man off any thought that he and Jamie were a couple. Eli got a raised eyebrow from Patrick and a sidewise glance from Jamie for his effort.

"Me, too, on Singles Plus on Thursdays," Becca said. "How does Tuesday sound?"

"That would work for me if we make the meeting at six, rather than seven," Tessa said. "Then I won't have to find someone for the eight o'clock movie showing. Gram could do it for me, but I hate to ask her to."

Everyone else agreed that would be okay.

"Tuesday week after next it is, then," Becca said.

The committee members rose and reached for their coats. Eli grabbed Jamie's as it started to slide to the floor.

"Thanks," she said, her pink-tinged lips curving up in a smile that waved over him like warm maple syrup. He enjoyed doing things for her, would like to do more if she'd let him.

She held her hand out for her jacket.

"Allow me," he said. A muffled chuckle from Anne reminded him they weren't alone.

Jamie slid her arms in, double time, and he released the coat, popping the warm bubble of emotion enclosing them.

"Payton, do you have a minute?" Patrick's voice ripped away the remainder of the bubble.

He glanced at Jamie, who had stepped away from the student desk and was approaching Becca. "I could." Eli didn't want to make whatever Patrick had to say easy for him.

Patrick looked past Eli to Jamie and the other woman. "Not here. We could get coffee at the diner."

Eli crossed his arms. "All right." Whatever Patrick wanted to say to him had to have something to do with Charlie and Brett, and he'd had about all he could take of her.

The two men strode toward the classroom door side by side as if in a synchronized race. Jamie held her breath waiting to see what would happen when they reached the doorway. At the last minute, Eli dropped back a step and allowed Patrick to exit first. The door closed behind Eli.

"Do you think I should call a hall monitor to break it up?" Becca asked, only half joking.

"The Russells aren't Eli's favorite people," Jamie said.

"So I've gathered." Becca fiddled with the button on her coat. "Mentioning that you and Eli were bowling together wasn't the only thing my mother-in-law—former mother-in-law—said. She also repeated some nasty gossip about Eli. And included you."

"I know." Jamie rubbed her forehead. "I was hoping that if Eli and I avoided being seen with each other, the gossip would die out."

"And with my pregnancy brain, I didn't even think about the problems having Patrick on the committee might cause for Eli."

"I feel badly for both of them, the trouble Charlotte is causing for Eli, and Patrick's marriage falling apart. He moved out several months ago." Jamie stopped. She'd forgotten Becca's husband, Matt, had left her at about the same time. When had she gotten so careless about other people's feelings? Until now, she'd hardly given a thought to how Charlotte's actions were hurting Eli, only to protecting her children and her reputation from the woman.

"I'd better get going." Becca filled the growing silence. "Or Matt's mother will be giving me another lecture about how little time I spend with Brendon."

"Yeah, I need to round my kids up from the basketball game."

The two women walked out into the hall where Anne was waiting for Jamie.

"I thought we could go down to the basketball game together," Anne said. "Autumn mentioned to her dad that she was taking your kids, so Neal decided to bring Ian."

"The twins, too?"

Anne laughed. "No, I don't think the Schroon Lake Wildcats are ready for the twins yet. Neal's parents are watching them."

"Well, I'll leave you ladies to your basketball game." Becca said goodbye and left.

"Now we can catch up," Anne said. "Since we're not next door neighbors anymore, it seems like I never see you."

"I know what you mean." A hollow formed in Jamie's stomach. She and Anne had been close, but after John had died and she'd stopped going to church and the Singles Plus group, they hadn't gotten together much.

"Eli and Patrick sure shot out of the meeting fast," Anne said. "I'd planned to ask Eli if he wanted to join us at the game. He and Neal are old friends. They went to high school here. Patrick, too."

But Jamie was sure Eli didn't consider Patrick an old friend.

Anne's expression turned thoughtful. "You haven't

lived here much longer than I have. Do you ever feel like you're out of the loop, the only one without a script? Don't get me wrong, everyone—well, almost everyone—is really nice, but it seems like they've all know each other since birth."

"Yes, all those little details that aren't filled in because everyone else knows them. Like, Leah Summers and I were friends for a couple of years, but I had no idea she was Eli's mother until I ran into them together at the hardware store. She always called him JR."

And she'd known Charlotte just as long. Katy had been the first friend Rose had made when they'd moved here. But, while she'd quickly learned Charlotte was a gossip, she had no idea she could be so vicious. Or, until that day at her house, that Eli had such a history with Charlotte and, apparently, with Patrick.

"So." Anne's voice dropped. "Did I pick up something between you and Eli?"

Evidently, Anne hadn't heard the gossip. Maybe it was dying down or wasn't as widespread as Jamie had feared.

"Come on," Anne coaxed, "you can tell me. You knew about Neal and me before I knew about Neal and me."

"No, there isn't. Not really." *Even though, if it weren't so complicated, if there wasn't a chance the*

Guard could call him to active duty at any time, a
part of me might like there to be.

Eli and Patrick arrived at the diner at the same
time and sat at a table in the corner, rather than at
the counter. While they waited for the waitress, Eli
took the offensive. "You had something you wanted
to talk about."

Patrick turned his head from side to side, scoping
out the late dinner customers. "I wanted to thank
you."

"Hi, Mr. Payton."

Sara, one of his senior students, stood next to the
table, an order pad in her hand.

"What can I get you?"

"Just coffee."

"And you?" she asked Patrick.

"The same."

She started to flip the page of the pad.

"One check," Eli said. The interruption had
given him time to regroup. "Thank me for what?"
he asked once Sara was out of earshot.

"Helping Brett. I know there's no reason you
should. Given Charlie's behavior lately, you probably have several good reasons not to."

Eli couldn't disagree. "Brett seems like a good
kid." Eli shrugged. "I could help him. So I am. No
big deal."

Skepticism flickered in Patrick's eyes. "You know I would pay for his college."

"Yeah, Brett told me that, and that his mother doesn't want you to."

"I suppose he told you about her cockamamie scheme to sue you for back child support to pay for his college."

"He did."

Patrick shook his head and dropped his gaze to the tabletop. "Charlie… She's not well. She won't get help. That's why I moved out, to give Katy and Liam a break from her. I have them every other week, Tuesday through Wednesday, unless I'm traveling for work."

Eli wasn't sure why the guy was telling him all this. It wasn't as if they were close friends or had ever been close friends. "If you're asking me to cut her some slack, there's not much to cut. She's hurt people I care about."

"Here you go." Sara arrived with their coffee.

Patrick sat tight-lipped while Sara placed the mugs on the table and left. "Charlie has hurt a lot of people, but…" His voice was raw.

"You love her." Eli couldn't keep the surprise out of his voice.

"Yep, I still do."

It might have been the dim lighting in the diner, but slumped in the chair across from him, Patrick looked ten years older than he had at the committee meeting. "You know Charlie and I—"

"I know Brett is mine. He looks just like my brother, always has. And I'm sure Charlie knows, too, except when it suits her to pretend he isn't— like when she's mad and wants to get back at me for something I've done or when she's depressed and slips back in time. Then she wants to punish both of us for your not taking her away from Paradox Lake." Patrick shook his head slowly as if it were an effort. "I'd asked her to marry me before she found out she was pregnant. She put me off and then wouldn't give me an answer until you came home from basic training and refused to marry her. Now, as I said, she isn't well and is bringing it all up again."

"We never…that night at the Maple Shade Motel, we were drunk. We both fell asleep."

"We've come a long way since then, the three of us, haven't we?"

They had, but maybe not far enough.

"I'm not making excuses for Charlie. But the boys growing up—Brett moving out and Liam planning to go away to college—dredged up Charlie's old resentment about being stuck in Paradox Lake. Then, last year I was up for a promotion at the Memphis office until a corporate restructuring eliminated the position. Charlie had her heart set on moving to Tennessee."

"She always did want to get away from here, and I couldn't wait to come back."

"I didn't see it coming. I thought she was happy here until the possibility of the transfer came up. Things started to fall apart when it didn't happen." Patrick took a long draw on his coffee. "While I'm throwing things out, I know you're active in the Hazardtown Community Church. One of my co-workers has been preaching to me for years. Lately, it's been making sense. I was thinking about trying church, bringing Katy. She has friends who go to Sunday school there. Would I be welcome, well, because of Charlie?"

"Of course." *At least by most of the members.* "I'm not going to preach to you like your coworker, but would you like to pray together for Charlie?"

A muscle worked in Patrick's jaw.

"Or for me to pray for you and Charlie?"

"Yeah, it couldn't hurt."

As Eli drove home, he prayed for Patrick and Charlie and their kids, but somehow Jamie kept slipping into those prayers. He turned into his driveway. Maybe it was time he did something about that.

Chapter Eleven

"Mom, are you going out again tonight?" Opal whined before Jamie had even gotten all of the way in the door from work the next Friday. You'd think she was out every night, rather than the one night a week she went bowling.

Before she could answer, her cell phone rang. "Hello."

"Jamie, this is Eli."

Her coat slipped from her hand as she was hanging it on one of the hooks by the kitchen. She hadn't recognized the phone number. Eli had always called her from school before.

"Karen asked me to call you."

Her heart slowed. It was about bowling. What else would it be?

"If you haven't heard, there was a fire in the kitchen at the bowling alley last night."

"No, I hadn't." She secured her coat on the hook. "Was it bad?"

"Not too bad, mostly smoke damage. But the lanes won't be open for a couple weeks while they clean up."

"Oh, okay. Thanks for letting me know."

"Wait. Do you already have a babysitter for tonight?"

"Myles was going to watch Rose and Opal." *If I decided to go to bowling.* "Why?"

"I still owe you that cheeseburger special."

She smiled to herself, the remembrance of the morning they'd installed the insulation blocking out the embarrassment of their conversation at church. She couldn't believe she'd let her bitterness about John slip out. "I thought we'd agreed, no cheeseburger special," she said, wanting back the easy companionship that had been growing between them before the incident with Charlotte.

"We could renegotiate. When I was at the diner last week, I noticed it has a cheeseburger special on Friday nights, too."

Was Eli asking her out? That didn't exactly fit their agreement to avoid being seen together.

"Are you still there?" he asked.

"Yeah, I'm here. You're asking me out to dinner?"

"No."

Her heart dropped as she went back over their conversation to see what she'd misconstrued.

"That debt for your treating me to lunch at your

place is weighing heavy on me. I like to pay my debts promptly."

She burst out laughing. "You don't owe me, Eli, really. And I just got home from the birthing center." She searched her mind for more reasons to put him off.

"I'll give you an hour to get the kids ready and wind down. You were planning to go bowling, right?"

"Yes."

"Great, I'll be there at six. See you then." He clicked off.

Jamie stared at her phone. It looked like she'd just agreed to go out to dinner with Eli. She turned to Opal. "Yes, I'm going out."

Eli sat in his truck a moment before getting out to walk to Jamie's door. He'd been a little pushy with her, but he didn't want to give her a chance to say no. He breathed in and released the breath in a frosty cloud before knocking at the door. It opened, but at first he didn't see anyone.

"Hi, Mr. Payton."

He looked down. "Hi, Opal. Are you supposed to be opening the door?"

"I looked out the window first and knew it was you. I know your truck."

The clatter of dishes echoed from the dining room. Jamie must be cleaning up from the kids' dinner, something Eli thought the kids could do themselves. But he wouldn't say that to Jamie. "Would you tell your mother I'm here?"

"She's not ready yet because she had to make us dinner. I told her I didn't like her going out. But it's really because I don't like what Myles cooks. So, Mommy said she'd make us something." Opal plopped herself down on the couch. "That was before I knew she was going out with you. I don't mind her going out with you."

"Opal, ask *him* to sit down, and get back in here and help Rose clear the table," Myles called from the other room.

Obviously not everyone was as agreeable as Opal about him and Jamie going out.

"I gotta ask him something first, Myles," she shouted back. "Brothers!"

"What did you want to ask me?"

She looked up at Eli, a miniature version of her mother.

"Since you and Mommy are going out now, does that mean you can take Rose and me to the dinner-dance? It's next Saturday, you know."

"That would be up to your mother."

"What would be up to her mother?" Jamie walked across the room to them. His heart thumped with each step. She wore the same light purple sweater she'd had on the day they'd insulated the attic—before she'd changed into her Buffalo Bills sweatshirt—and fitted slacks that showed off her attractive figure.

"Whether he can take us to the dinner-dance now that he's your boyfriend," Opal explained.

A blush tinged Jamie's cheeks. "Aren't you supposed to be helping Rose and Myles with the dishes?"

"But you didn't answer."

"Go." Jamie pointed to the doorway.

"You can call me tomorrow and tell me what Mommy says. She can give you the number," Opal called over her shoulder as she scooted away to the dining room.

Eli struggled to keep a straight face until the little girl had disappeared into the other room. Then he looked at Jamie and they both burst out laughing. "She doesn't give up, does she?"

"Never."

"I could take them. I don't have any plans for next Saturday."

Jamie raised her face to him, all traces of her laughter gone.

He should have kept his mouth shut.

"Let's go to dinner and I'll think about it."

"You could come, too. I could take all three of you."

"For cheeseburgers? No, the girls have already eaten."

"I didn't mean…" He stopped when he caught the gleam in her eyes. "Got me."

He lifted her coat from her arm and held it for her. A light floral scent tickled his nose, enticing him to lean closer. She turned her head and he drew back, but not before he noticed the flash of sparkle on her ears. Jamie's date-night earrings, Opal had said the last time he was here. A good sign that she had accepted his invitation as a date.

"Thanks." Her smile lit her face and his heart.

Jamie was surprised at how busy the diner was. The winter months drew far fewer tourists than the warmer ones. She'd expected only another family or two, not for almost every table to be taken.

"The food here must be really good," Eli said. "Look at the people."

Jamie looked around again. He didn't need to remind her how crowded it was. Crowded with people she knew from the birthing center, from the school when she worked there, from the kids' activities. Family people. All of whom would see her and Eli together.

"What's wrong?" Eli asked.

"Nothing." She covered her concern with a short laugh that came out more like a cough. "I'm just surprised to see half the population of Schroon Lake *and* Paradox Lake here."

"A regular Friday night family hot spot."

Her tension ebbed. Eli was right. It was a family place, not a romantic spot, the kind of restaurant where good friends might go for a meal. Friends like her and Eli.

"Hi," the hostess greeted them. "Booth or table?"

Eli looked at her.

"Table, please," Jamie said. The kids always insisted on a booth when she took them out. Tonight was Friday, her adult night out.

"You're going to have to wait awhile. All we have free right now are booths, unless you want to sit at the counter."

"No, not the counter." She felt as if all the eyes in the room were on her and Eli standing here. Eating front and center at the counter would be worse.

"A booth will be fine, more private." Eli took the final decision from her. He shrugged. "What can I say? I'm hungry."

"This way, please." The hostess led them to a booth a short distance away.

Jamie slid down the bench on one side of the table. A booth *was* a better choice. The walls offered privacy. Eli sat across from her.

"Your waitress will be with you in a minute." The hostess handed a menu to each of them.

Eli flipped open his menu. "You don't have to get the cheeseburger special."

Jamie rubbed her finger along the edge of her menu. His insistence on treating her to anything she wanted felt too datelike to her. They weren't on a date. They were friends having dinner together.

"You don't have to buy my dinner. Why don't we split the bill?"

"Hey, no reneging now. You said I could buy you the cheeseburger special. Besides, call me old-fashioned, but I think a man should pay for a date."

The teenage waitress approached their booth. "Hi, Mr. Payton."

"Hi, Sara."

"And Mrs. Glasser, Myles's mother, right? You were at the sledding party. Your little girls are so cute."

"Thank you."

"Are you ready to order?"

After Sara had taken their orders, Jamie unrolled the silverware. She didn't know what had gotten into her. She'd wanted to come tonight, and deep down she knew the evening was a date, despite her rationalization to herself. And she shouldn't be surprised he took charge. That was Eli. But when he'd said they'd take a booth, something clicked inside her and put up a wall of resistance. Truth was she wouldn't mind someone else being in charge for a few hours for a change.

"So, how was your week?" she asked. That seemed like a neutral enough topic.

"Busy. With midyear Regents exams over, I had some parent conferences I'd have preferred not to. Other than that I've been working on ideas for

Career Day, and the rifle class I'm teaching at the American Legion has started."

Jamie smoothed the napkin on her lap. The rifle class that Myles had begged her to let him take. "I've started working on my booth, too. The Medical Center public relations officer is sending me some materials from job fairs she's done in the area and pamphlets to hand out."

"Sounds good."

No, it didn't sound good. It sounded stilted and boring. Why was she having so much trouble talking with Eli and enjoying herself? Could be she was just plain out of practice socializing. She'd shut herself off these past twenty months. And—she looked at Eli, the masculine jut of his square jaw, the fine line of his patrician nose, his long fingers with their squared off nails flicking the edge of the paper placemat—she hadn't been on a date with a man other than John since she was sixteen years old.

Sara reappeared with their drinks. "Here you go, hot chocolate and coffee." She placed them in front of Jamie and Eli. "Your dinners will be out soon."

"Thanks," Jamie said, thankful for the interruption to the growing silence.

"Thanks," Eli echoed.

Silence fell over them again when Sara left. What was it that all those women's magazines she used to read recommended? Get the guy to talk about himself. Not that that had ever worked with John. He was more of the strong, silent type, even more so with every deployment to the Middle East.

"Tell me about yourself." She slid her cocoa mug an inch closer. That sounded as if they'd just met each other. But in a way they had. This was the first time they'd planned something together, just the two of them.

He shrugged. "Not a lot to tell that you probably don't already know from my mother. I grew up on Paradox Lake. My dad was a trucker, killed in an accident the winter I was fourteen. I joined the Air Force right out of high school with a lot of encouragement from Sheriff Norton after a 'harmless' prank some of the guys and I pulled turned out not to be so harmless."

She sipped her cocoa. So, Charlotte—or escaping Charlotte—wasn't the reason he'd joined the service.

"I started out in tactical aircraft maintenance, flew a few missions over the Desert, did that stint on the recruiting team and, after I'd gotten my college degrees nights and weekends whenever I could pick up a class, I finished off as an instructor at Maxwell Air Force Base. Now, here I am." He lifted his arms and spread his hands wide over the table, almost hitting Sara, who'd returned with their food.

"Cheeseburger special." Sara set Jamie's plate in front of her. "And rib eye steak. Do you need anything else?"

"No, we're good," Eli said with a wide smile before Jamie could open her mouth to say the same.

"Okay, let me know if you do," Sara said before she left.

Jamie breathed in the tantalizing aroma of grilled beef. "I don't mind if you want to go ahead and say grace." She waited in surprisingly comfortable silence while he briefly bowed his head.

"Now," he said, "it's your turn to spill. I've known most of the people around here for, well, always. But you're not from Paradox Lake." He stated the obvious.

"Funny. Anne Hazard and I were talking about that. How everyone seems to know everyone. Sometimes we feel like we're at play practice without a script."

He laughed. "My script on you is blanker than I'd like. How'd you end up in Paradox Lake?"

"Anne's husband, Neal. He was a friend of John's. John was stationed at Fort Drum and Neal's National Guard unit trained there. When John's unit deployed time before last, I wanted to get back into nursing but had trouble finding a job that worked out with the kids. Neal let me know when the school nurse job opened up at Schroon Lake Central." Jamie took a bite of her burger and swallowed. "That's where I worked before the birthing center."

Eli nodded. "And where'd you grow up?"

"A suburb of Buffalo, a place much larger than

Paradox Lake. My folks still live there. I thought about going back after John's death. My parents wanted me to. But the area has gotten kind of rough. Paradox Lake is a better place for kids. Safer." After losing John, she wanted to keep them out of harm's way was as best she could.

"Paradox Lake is a good place to grow up. I can vouch for that."

"And we like it here, even though Myles claims he's out of here the minute he graduates high school."

The rest of the meal passed quickly with them sharing stories of their childhoods.

"Are you ready for dessert?" Sara asked when she came over to pick up their finished plates.

"None for me," Jamie said.

"I'd like a piece of the apple pie I saw on the menu and more coffee."

"Coffee sounds good to me, too," Jamie said.

Rather than digging into his pie when it arrived, Eli tapped the flakey crust with his fork, weighing whether or not to tell Jamie about the paternity test results. They *had* been talking about the past and filling in the blanks. He looked across the table. She ran her fingertips around the rim of her coffee mug, a soft half smile on her face. His vocal chords froze.

Eli cleared his throat. Might as well get it over with, even though it would probably mean an end to the evening. He owed it to her. Letting her know had been the reason he'd asked her out tonight. One of his reasons. The others had had more to do with the way her dark curls caressed the sweet curve of her cheek, how she moved her graceful, capable hands to emphasize a point when she spoke and her fierce-mother protectiveness over her kids.

"If you were one of my kids, I'd ask you whether you were going to eat that pie or play with it," Jamie teased.

"I'm going to eat it. Definitely. But first I have something I want to tell you."

Jamie set her coffee mug down and looked at him intently.

"I got the results of the paternity test." He didn't see any need to tell her what the results were.

She wrapped her hands around the mug as if she needed to hang on to something and trained her eyes on his face.

He swallowed. "I called Charlie and went over to talk with her Wednesday night when the kids weren't there. They go to Patrick's every other week."

Jamie nodded. She probably knew that from Rose and Katy being friends.

"Charlie seemed to take it okay. She didn't make any kind of scene." As he'd feared she might. "She just got quiet and looked very tired."

"So that's taken care of," Jamie said in an even, almost monotone voice that struck him as out of character for the vibrant woman he'd come to know.

"I called Patrick when I got home. We'd talked about Charlie and Brett over coffee at the diner after the Career Day committee meeting last week. Patrick said Charlie isn't well. He's trying to convince her to get help." He knew he was running on, but he needed to see some reaction from Jamie. "Patrick agreed I'd done the right thing. For everyone. He's been concerned about the kids."

Jamie's uplifted face was a blank slate.

He should just stop, but he couldn't. He needed to see some emotion from her. His past had hurt Jamie and her family. "Patrick called me this morning and said Charlie had seemed okay when he'd brought Katy and Liam back later that night, calmer than he'd seen her in a while." He caught his breath. "And that Brett had said she seemed fine when he'd stopped in at the hardware store to see her yesterday."

"Thank you for telling me." She shifted her gaze away from his.

Yes, he'd torpedoed the evening. But it was better that she hear it from him. He mumbled a "You're welcome" and attacked the pie, which tasted like wet cardboard.

"More coffee, cocoa?" Sara asked as she breezed by with another table's order.

"Not for me." Jamie placed her hand over her mug.

"I'm fine, too." Actually, far from it. But he had had enough coffee.

"I'll get your check, then," Sara said.

"I appreciate your telling me," Jamie repeated, breaking the silence Sara's departure had left. She twisted the paper napkin she'd taken from her lap, her eyes meeting his again, almost as if she'd made some kind of decision.

He held his breath, waiting for her to kick him to the curb.

"I know Charlotte's actions weren't your fault."

His heart lightened. "They were, in a way. I did some things I'm not proud of. If—"

Jamie interrupted before he could say more. "That was a long time ago. It's just that Charlotte hurt my kids."

"I know, and for that I'm sorry." One thing he'd learned about Jamie was that she protected her kids with the ferocity of a lioness.

Her lips curved up. "I think I know of a way you could right some of it, with the girls, at least."

Was that a glint in her eye?

"You could take Opal and Rose to the dinner-dance at school."

It was a glint, definitely a glint.

"Believe me," she said. "That's more of a payback than you might think."

"I think I can handle it. On one condition."

"And what would that be?"

"You have to come, too."

"I'll have to take that up with the girls."

All right, then. Opal liked him. Rose seemed to as well. Maybe he hadn't totally blown things with Jamie.

Chapter Twelve

"Don't I look beautiful?" Opal asked, spinning around in the middle of the living room so that her skirt flared.

"You do," Jamie agreed. "And you, too, Rose. You look so grown-up."

Jamie had taken them shopping last Saturday. Opal had chosen a gauzy dress with a full skirt embroidered with small flowers that she called a fairy dress. Rose had found a turquoise dress in a lacy fabric over a satin underdress that was gathered at the waist and fell softly to just above her knees.

It was far too dressy for Rose's usual wear. But her big blue eyes—her father's eyes—had gone wide the moment she'd spotted it. *Funny, Rose was the only one of the kids who had John's blue eyes.* Jamie couldn't say no. And she'd let Rose get sheer tights that looked almost like stockings. Rose, her more reserved middle child, sometimes seemed to get lost in the shadows. Jamie had wanted to get her something special.

"Thanks, Mom. You look pretty hot, too, for a mother," Rose said. "You haven't worn that dress in a long time."

Jamie rubbed the fabric of the tea-length cocktail dress between her thumb and forefinger. She'd only worn it once, for her parents' fortieth anniversary party the fall after John had been killed. She'd bought it for her and John's date night, as the kids called their infrequent evenings out, to celebrate his return. She dropped the fabric as if it burned and checked the clock to see if she had time to change into something more comfortable. A crunch of tires on the driveway told her no.

"I'll get the door," Opal said and opened it before Eli had even reached the top step of the porch.

Eli had traded his familiar ski jacket for a double-breasted wool dress coat. Brushing the dusting of snow off his shoulders, he stomped his feet on the welcome mat before stepping in.

"We're all ready," Opal announced, gesturing from herself to Rose to her mother.

"So I see, and you're all..." He fastened his gaze on Jamie. "Lovely." His voice dropped on the last word, sending a ripple of pleasure through her.

"I'm a lucky guy to be going out with three such beautiful women."

"You're silly. Mommy is the only woman. Rose and I are just girls."

Eli smiled.

"Go get your coats," Jamie said, sending Rose and Opal to the other room. "You do realize what you've gotten yourself into with Opal as your 'date'?" Jamie walked across the room, opened the front closet and removed a caramel-colored car coat with faux shearling lining and collar.

As Eli helped her put the coat on, she couldn't help comparing her department store special to his finely tailored coat. It shouldn't bother her. She was a single parent with three kids to support.

"I hadn't realized I was exclusively Opal's date. I thought I was escorting all three of you."

"No," Jamie said firmly, closing the last button and looking up into Eli's steel-blue eyes inches from hers. "To hear Opal, you're taking *her* to the dinner-dance and Rose and I are kind of tag-alongs, particularly me. She's not at all sure why I need to come except, maybe, to keep Rose company."

"And so I have some adult company." His gaze held hers and she breathed the spicy scent of winter mixed with a subtle men's cologne.

Jamie released a rusty laugh. "Or for protection from Opal and her incessant questions. I'm sure she has a select few saved up for tonight."

"Nope," he said, shaking his head without breaking his gaze. "That one didn't make my list."

* * *

Eli held the school cafeteria door open for Jamie and the girls and followed them in. Someone had been busy this afternoon, moving the tables to a ring around the edges to open up a dance area complete with a DJ stand manned by a couple of the senior boys. He scanned the room and checked his watch, glancing over at Jamie to see if she was watching him. Her comment the other day had made him conscious of how time-focused he was. He relaxed. She was helping Opal take her coat off.

It was a great turnout. At least twenty of the possible forty elementary school girls were here with their various escorts.

"Mr. Payton," Rose said. "We're supposed to put our coats on the table over there." She pointed to the far left side of the cafeteria.

"I was going to tell him that," Opal said.

Jamie shot her a pointed look and Opal didn't say any more, although the frown on her face clearly stated her feelings. Apparently, only she was supposed to talk to him.

Eli slipped his coat off, realizing they'd already removed theirs. "I'll take them over." He crossed the room, saying hello to several teachers who were there and parents he knew. He placed the coats on the table, with his on top.

"Eli, I didn't expect to see you here."

He turned to face Brett Russell. Eli hadn't expected to see him, either. He glanced across the room to see if Jamie was looking this way. She was talking to Rose's teacher.

"I'm filling in for Dad," Brett said. He jerked his head toward the dark-haired girl standing next to him. Eli remembered seeing his sister, Katy, at Jamie's house. "Grandma took a fall this afternoon, and he had to take her up to the Medical Center in Saranac Lake."

"I hope she's okay."

"She might have broken her hip."

"Sorry. I'll say a prayer for her fast recovery."

"Thanks. Grandma's pretty tough."

"Yep, that's what I remember. She had to be to keep your dad and your four uncles in line."

"Brett!" Katy tugged on the teen's hand. "There's Rose and her mother. We've got to get over there so we can get a table with them before they sit with Opal's friends."

"I guess I've got to move on."

"Right," Eli said. He did, too, but uncertainty about how Jamie would react to Brett joining them made him pause. "I'll walk over with you."

"Sure. Are you here as a chaperone?"

"Not exactly."

Opal met them halfway across the room. "Mr. Payton, we have to get our table now."

"Hi, Opal," Katy said. "We were coming over to sit with you guys."

"Hi, Katy. Where's your dad?" Opal smiled up at Eli. "Mr. Payton brought us."

Brett gave him a sideways glance.

"Dad had to take Grandma to the hospital. My brother Brett brought me."

Opal's mouth formed an *O* as she looked from Eli to Brett.

Eli rubbed the back of his neck, remembering the questions Jamie had told him Opal had asked about Brett and him.

"Oh, there's Amy." She looked up at Eli. "She's my best friend. I want her to sit with us, too. Take Katy and her brother over to Mommy. She's getting us a table."

"Katy!" Rose waved and called them over.

Katy raced ahead.

"So," Brett said, "you brought Katy's friend Rose and her sister? I thought you and their mother weren't…"

"We weren't." Eli cut him off and glanced at Jamie. But now maybe they were? "Opal, that's Rose's sister, has kind of latched on to me. She decided I should bring her to the dinner-dance and that was that."

Brett knitted his brow. "Ah, okay, if you say so."

Eli looked away. Who did he think he was fooling? He was here with Jamie.

* * *

"Hi, Katy," Jamie said. "Rose saved you the seat next to her. Where's your dad?"

"He couldn't come."

Jamie grasped the hard plastic back of the cafeteria chair she was pulling out for herself. "So." The word came out as more of a croak. "Are you here with your mother?" How was she going to sit at a table all evening with Eli and Charlotte?

"Nope," she said as she slid into the chair next to Rose. "She wasn't feeling good."

Jamie felt only a small pang of guilt at the relief the little girl's answer had brought.

"My brother Brett brought me."

Jamie collapsed in the chair she'd pulled out for herself. Brett sitting with them would only be incrementally less uncomfortable for Eli than having Charlotte there with them. And where were Eli and Opal? She hoped her darling daughter wasn't dragging him around the room like some kind of prize to show off.

"Mommy." Opal came up from behind and startled her. "I found Amy." She led her friend and a pleasant-looking man about Jamie's age to the other side of the table.

"Hi," the man said. "I'm Scott Murray."

"Jamie Glasser, Opal and Rose's mother, as you've probably figured out."

Eli and Brett joined them, and Opal directed

everyone to their seats, putting Brett between her mother and Katy and Eli next to her, across the table from Jamie.

Eli extended his hand to Scott and introduced himself and Brett.

"I'm here with Amy," Scott said. "I take it you're Opal's date."

"Yes, I'm Opal and Rose's date," Eli said with a wide grin that emphasized his cheekbones and the slight hollows beneath them.

Scott smiled at Jamie over Opal's head.

She remembered Opal saying that Amy's mother's boyfriend would be bringing Amy to the dance. Jamie forced a smile back. *Scott must think Eli and I are together, along with everyone else here I know from school.*

Jamie watched Eli settle into the cafeteria chair. His motions were fluid and relaxed, as if Brett's presence had no effect on him. She had that "no-script" feeling she and Anne had talked about again.

"You look familiar," Scott said to Brett. "Do you go to North Country? I teach math there."

"I do. But I hope to get into the Air Force Academy. Eli is coaching me."

Jamie looked across at Eli, who immediately dropped his gaze and ran his finger over a scratch on the table. Another page missing from the script. But who was she to expect him to share everything he did with her? They'd gone on one date, and for half of it she'd pretended it wasn't a date.

"Eli is retired Air Force," Brett filled in for the confused-looking Scott. "I figured, since I'm not applying right out of high school, I need all the help I can get. He's my brother's guidance counselor."

"Here at the high school," Eli added.

"Attention everyone," the teacher who was serving as MC for the evening said. "The buffet is ready. We'll start with Mr. Payton's table." The teacher pointed at them. "And go clockwise."

While Jamie was glad for something to do, she wasn't so glad to find everyone looking at them.

Opal pulled Eli from his chair.

"Wait for your mom."

"Go ahead." This was the girls' night. Rose was fine hanging out with Katy, and Opal was in her glory with Eli. She really hadn't needed to come. But Eli had insisted.

"See, Mommy says it's okay."

If Jamie had been in a less self-pitying mood, she would have laughed at the torn expression on Eli's face.

She nodded to him and he escorted Opal to the buffet table.

"Looks like we've been ditched," Brett said beside her, lifting his chin toward Rose and his sister, Katy. He tipped the chair in front of him back and forth as if unsure how she'd take his quip.

"It's not the first time."

Brett frowned at Eli's back, and she hastily added, "That the girls have chosen a friend over me."

"Yeah. We should get in line." Brett stepped back from the table so she could pass by him.

His polite expression had a bit of a lost look about it that touched Jamie's motherly side. He was an adult, but just barely. And if she felt a little unneeded here tonight, he must feel even more out of place.

"Thanks," she said with what she hoped was a reassuring smile. She thought his brother, Liam, was a bad influence on Myles and hadn't been prepared to like Brett.

Dinner passed quickly with Eli and the other men including her in their conversation, which centered on school talk and the next weekend's NFL games. Soon, the high school DJ was announcing the first dance. Eli danced to a fast song with Opal, and then with Rose, while Jamie worked at keeping her smile under control. She'd discovered something Eli was not good at. He sat out the next one, pleading a need to rest, and the girls danced with their girlfriends. Then the DJ put on a slow song.

"Would you like to dance?" Eli asked.

"Go ahead, Mommy," Opal said before Jamie could get her mouth open. "Rose and I already danced with Mr. Payton. It's your turn."

Something in the way Eli's gaze rested on her

face made her feel he wasn't asking because it was her turn. She took a breath to calm the flip-flop in her stomach. "I'd love to."

The smile he gave her in return undid any calming her cleansing breath had achieved. He walked around the table and took her hand. When they reached the makeshift dance floor, he placed his other hand on the small of her back and glided into the song with his usual athletic grace.

To fend off the nervous energy building in her from the pleasure of dancing with Eli and the feeling people were looking at them, she searched for a conversation topic other than her kids or football. "It was nice of you to help Brett." She let her curiosity get the best of her.

Eli guided her smoothly to the right to avoid another couple. "No big deal. The Lord says we should use our talents. I could help, so I did."

That was so Eli. Jamie allowed herself to relax in the strength of his arms and not think about what that characteristic could mean to their budding relationship.

"You really like working with kids, don't you?"

He twirled her around. "I do. During my last few years teaching at Maxwell, I looked forward to each new round of recruits."

Jamie stiffened. Young men and women, each some mother's child, being trained to face danger. Maybe Eli's helping Brett wasn't such a nice thing.

"Hey." Eli's breath caressed her hair. "I didn't mess up my lead, did I? I know I didn't step on your foot."

"No." She relaxed and let him lead her in flow with the music. "You're a great dancer. Slow dancer." She corrected herself.

He laughed, soft and low, strumming a chord deep inside her. "I know my limitations. You don't need to remind me."

"But Rose and Opal loved it, and I'm sure they're ready for more."

"That's what's important. It is their night."

Jamie moved a little closer to him and let the music drown out her earlier feeling of being left out. And for the moment, she pretended it was her night, too.

An hour and a half and two slow dances later, Eli pulled Jamie's car up next to his truck in her driveway. "Do you want me to put it in the garage?"

"Yes, please." Jamie lifted the remote from the console between the front seats and opened the garage door so Eli could drive in.

Eli jumped out and walked around to open Jamie's door for her first, then the back door for Rose and Opal. He walked them all to the front door.

"Thank Mr. Payton for the evening," Jamie said.

"Thanks, Mr. Payton," they said in unison.

"I had a nice time, too," Jamie said.

"So did I." His gaze pinned hers.

She reached for the doorknob.

"Rose and Opal, you go ahead in. I want to talk with your mother for a minute."

"It's cold out here. You should come in and talk. Mommy could make us cocoa," Opal said.

"Opal, don't you know anything?" Rose said. "He doesn't want to talk. He wants to kiss Mom goodnight, like in the movies."

Jamie felt her cheeks heat.

"Actually, I do want to talk with your mother."

She opened the door for the girls, glad for something to do to counteract the nonsensical letdown Eli's words had brought.

"What's up?" A twinge of dread tweaked Jamie. She couldn't think of anything Eli wouldn't want to say in front of the girls, except something about Myles and school or something about Brett and Charlotte.

"What I wanted to say is that I've been waiting all evening to do this." He bent his head and pressed his lips to hers. Heart thrumming, she placed her hands on his shoulders for balance and kissed him back.

Too soon, he lifted his head, breaking the kiss. Frosty air filled the space that opened between them. She shivered, not entirely from the wintry weather. "I'd better get in."

"Good night," he said softly before he turned and walked to his truck.

She touched her lips with her gloved fingers. Stars twinkled in the inky sky above. For once, she couldn't argue with Eli. It was a good night. One of the best ones she'd had in a good long time.

Chapter Thirteen

Jamie glanced at the clock for the third time in five minutes. Where was Myles? He was supposed to be home from working at Hill's Auto twenty minutes ago. Eli would be here anytime to pick her up for the Career Day committee meeting. She pushed her hair back from her forehead. Why had she agreed to let Myles help Jack at the garage on a school night, especially when she needed Myles to watch Rose and Opal?

She paced the room. She'd been in too good of a mood, looking forward to going to the meeting, to say no to Myles. Her stomach churned. She didn't even know if Myles was at Hill's, not that he'd done anything recently to make her distrust him. She grabbed the house phone from the charger and dialed the garage number. The phone rang and rang, her anger and frustration growing with each ring.

"Hill's Auto Repair," Jack answered.

"Hi, this is Jamie. Is Myles there?" She rocked on the balls of her feet, waiting for the answer.

"Yeah, he's right here doing an oil change for me."

"Didn't he tell you that he had to be home by six-thirty to watch Rose and Opal?" Jamie knew it wasn't Jack's fault. She was sure Jack would have brought Myles home if Myles had told him. But she couldn't keep the anger out of her voice.

"No, he didn't. Sorry. Myles finished putting the parts away and I had this oil change to do. He was really psyched that I'd let him do it."

She had no doubts Myles would be psyched, but that didn't help her.

"Do you want me to bring him home now?"

Jamie pushed her hair back from her forehead. "Yes, please, if you would."

She ended the call and started to punch in Eli's cell phone number, hoping to catch him and tell him not to stop for her. No sense in them both being late, and she did not want Eli here when Myles got home. Before she could finish, her cell phone started playing the old Three Dog Night song "Eli's Coming," one of her mother's favorite classic rock songs. Jamie had programmed it in for Eli's ringtone.

"Hey." The low masculine timber soothed her fraying nerves. "I'm just leaving the house now. Mom called as I was heading for the door."

"That's okay. I was about to call you. I'm running late. You might as well go over without me. I'll drive myself."

"You okay? You sound funny."

She warmed at his concern. "Yes, Myles lost track of time. He was helping Jack Hill at the garage after school today, and he's not home yet." Better to let Eli think that than voicing her suspicion that Myles had done it on purpose.

"I can run over and get him."

"No need. I talked with Jack and they're on their way."

"All right. I'll see you at school."

Thirty minutes and a good dressing-down of Myles later, Jamie rushed to Becca's classroom. Myles had said that he'd gotten caught up in the job and hadn't been watching the time. She wasn't at all sure she believed him, since Jack had said he didn't know anything about Myles having to be home by six-thirty.

She turned the doorknob and pushed the door in. Everyone turned and looked at her. "Sorry I'm late. Family stuff."

"We know," Becca said. "Eli filled us in."

It made no sense, and she knew it was because of Myles, but she couldn't help feeling put out at Eli for sharing whatever details he'd shared.

Jamie slipped off her coat and sat at the empty desk between Eli and Anne. He handed her Becca's meeting agenda.

"We were brainstorming about getting the freshmen and sophomores more involved in Career Day, and Eli threw out one suggestion—have an American Legion booth."

"I'm not sure I understand. Do they hire students part-time?" She tried to imagine what they might hire students for. Yard work? Or maybe as wait staff for their Friday-night dinners. Neither sounded like much of a draw.

"No, but they have—"

"Let me explain," Eli interrupted Becca.

Jamie waited for him to add, "It was my idea," and then chided herself for being so peevish. It certainly wasn't Eli's fault that she and Myles had had another run-in.

"The American Legion has family and youth programs that can help teens prepare to choose a career."

"A military career." Jamie's flat tone made her opinion of the military clear, an opinion that she was well aware was in the minority here. But if John hadn't joined the army, he'd still be here, and her life would be different, easier. Her conscience pricked her. Would it be easier? She looked at Eli and waited for the usual feeling of betrayal to kick in. She couldn't deny that she was attracted to him, despite their differences and her fear he might inadvertently influence Myles to follow through with his threat to enlist when he graduated. But the feeling of betrayal didn't come, throwing her further off-kilter.

"No, not necessarily," Eli said in a calm, authoritative manner she was sure he'd honed through his youth work. A manner she'd seemed to have lost lately dealing with Myles—if she'd ever had it.

"It sponsors Scouts, 4-H groups, Explorers and sports teams."

"Then why don't we have those groups sponsor booths?" She waited for some of the other committee members to comment. "I mean, doesn't it seem to anyone else that the Career Day is being over-weighted toward military careers?" *Training kids to put their lives in danger.*

"I don't think so," Patrick said.

"Me, neither," Liz and Tessa said.

Anne didn't say anything, but Jamie had a strong feeling that was out of friendship because Anne truly understood Jamie's opposition, even if she didn't agree with it. Jamie tapped her forefinger on the desk. Why had she even come tonight? She wasn't in a good frame of mind. Maybe this was all a sign that she wasn't ready to be out and involved yet. Or, her inner voice said, God's reminder that good works weren't a substitute for believing in Him.

"I have an idea," Anne said. "Why don't we have a booth for youth programs, rather than limiting it to the American Legion?"

"Sounds good to me," Becca said. The others murmured their agreement.

Jamie slipped a glance at Eli to see if he was gloating. Of course he wasn't. He was nodding his agreement like everyone else.

The rest of the meeting went by in a blur, with Jamie staying on the sidelines.

Eli touched her shoulder as she gathered her things from the desk to leave. "Do you want to go to the diner for coffee or hot chocolate since we're in town anyway?"

Him remembering her fondness for hot chocolate lightened her mood a bit, although not enough to make her feel like socializing. Before she could say no, thanks, her cell phone chimed. "Excuse me. It may be the kids."

He nodded.

It wasn't the kids. It was her boss, Kelly. "Hello, what's up?"

"I know you're not on call today, but Kristy Minor is in labor and Maura has come down with some kind of bug." Maura was the midwife practice's other delivery nurse. "Can you cover, please?"

"I guess. Yes. I just need to line up someone to stay with the kids tonight."

"Great. We have time. I'll meet you at the center."

"All right. Bye."

"Work?" Eli asked.

"Yes, I'm going to have to take a rain check on

the hot chocolate." No need telling him she was going to say that anyway. "I have to cover a birth for the other delivery nurse. She's sick." Jamie glanced toward the door. "I need to catch Anne to see if she can take the girls and check with Tanner's mother to see if Myles can go over there." If she'd been on call, she'd have these arrangements all set up. Old resentment flared. She wouldn't be in this spot if John… He'd be here for the kids or she'd still be working days at the school.

"I'll stay with them."

"You'd do that?" The rush of adrenaline that had started when she'd gotten the call and her mind had begun ticking off her child-care options slowed. His offer made everything easier, something she wasn't used to.

"Sure."

"Before I take you up on your offer, I have to warn you there's a good chance I'll be gone all night. It's a first-time mother."

"I can handle it. I'll swing by my place and pick up clothes for school tomorrow and go over to your house."

Jamie remembered Eli's words when she'd said it was kind of him to help Brett. I could, so I did. Was this the same or not? Her mind replayed his good-night kiss after the dinner-dance, and she did her best to ignore the part of herself that hoped it was more than simply helping because he could.

* * *

Eli strode up the walk to the Glassers' front door and rang the bell. He tightened and loosened his grip on the gym bag he'd packed with his clothes. Jamie had said she was going to call Myles to tell him Eli was on his way. He didn't know how that went, but he was gearing up for the worst. To prepare, he shot off a quick prayer for the wisdom to deal with Myles without his growing fondness for Jamie clouding his judgment and him overstepping his boundaries.

The teen definitely was not in favor of him and Jamie dating, if that's what they were doing. But that wasn't up to Myles. It was between him and Jamie. Eli rang the bell again and the door swung open.

Myles stood there. "Mom said you were coming over. I don't know why. I can watch the girls."

Eli stepped in and closed the door. "Your mother asked me to come because she's a good mother. It's not that she doesn't think you could do it. It's that she doesn't want to saddle you with the responsibility." Unlike his mother, who wouldn't have even thought of that. "Or leave herself open to anyone questioning her parenting." Eli felt a small qualm remembering that when he'd first met Jamie, he'd done just that.

"Mr. Payton!" Opal raced in the room and wrapped her arms around his legs, stopping any comment the teen might have had.

"I'm going up to my room," Myles said. "That's where you'll be staying. I'll show you when the squirts go to bed at eight-thirty. Rose and Opal are supposed to be finishing up their homework in the dining room." Myles shot Opal a stern look before turning heel and heading upstairs.

"Come on." Opal grabbed his hand and pulled him toward the dining room. "I have my homework done. You can check it. Mommy always does."

Eli glanced up the stairs as they walked by. Once Opal and Rose were in bed, he was going to have a talk with Myles man-to-man.

"Hi, Mr. Payton." Rose was seated at a large oak table, her math book open and a paper in front of her.

"Hi, Rose." He'd been in the kitchen and the living room and upstairs, but he hadn't been in the dining room before. He glanced around the room taking in the matching china cabinet and hutch. His perusal stopped at a photo of a younger Jamie gazing at a man about the same age in an army uniform with a dreamy look in her eyes. His heart twisted. Her husband, John. Rose looked a lot like him, more so than Opal or Myles.

"These are my spelling words." Opal shoved a paper at him. "I wrote them three times. Now I need to study them. Mommy always asks me and I spell them out loud."

He took the sheet, glad for something else to look at. "Let's do it."

Rose looked up at him. "Can you ask her words in the living room? My math is kind of hard, and I need to concentrate."

"Sure thing," Eli said. "Do you want me to check it over when you're done?"

Indecision clouded Rose's eyes. "Myles said he would."

"Then it sounds like you have it covered. I'll quiz Opal on her spelling words." He walked Opal back into the living room and sat on the couch with her. They ran through her words with Opal carefully spelling each one correctly.

"Father." Eli read the last word.

"F-a-t-h-e-r," Opal said, looking up at him with wide, serious eyes. "My father's dead."

"Yes, I know."

"Myles and Rose get mad at me because I don't remember him too well."

"They just feel badly because they have good memories of him and want you to, too."

She tilted her head, one side of her mouth pulling down. "I think you'd be a good daddy."

Her words hit him smack in the middle of his gut. "I hope to be some day."

"I mean my daddy." She snuggled up to him and he put his arm around her shoulders. "I pray that every night, even though Mommy doesn't sit and listen to our prayers anymore. She says they don't do any good."

Eli's chest caved in. None of his counseling courses or experience had prepared him to respond to a seven-year-old saying she wanted him to be her daddy. He'd been trained to work with recruits and teens.

"That's not going to happen, is it?" Opal asked. "Like Mommy says, God can't really give you what you ask for."

Eli swallowed back the flash of anger that Jamie would discourage her daughter's belief. A wave of sadness flowed over him and filled the gulf that separated him and Jamie spiritually.

For with God all things are possible. The end of Mark 10:27 blanked out his other thoughts. But he couldn't let Opal think that if she wished it hard enough, he would be her father. "We pray to God and He gives us what's best for us because He loves us."

"Like Mommy."

"Yes, a lot like your mother and my mother, too." Although he hadn't always appreciated her efforts.

"I'm all done." Rose's appearance in the room gave Eli a welcome interruption. "I'm going to give Myles my paper to check, and then Opal and I get to watch TV."

"Yep, we do," Opal agreed. "Ask Myles."

"What?" the teen asked from the bottom of the stairway behind them.

Rose walked over and handed him her homework paper. "You told Mom you'd check my problems. And Mr. Payton said to ask you if we can watch TV now that our homework is done."

"Yeah, Mom lets them watch some show on Nickelodeon before they have to go to bed," Myles said, his eyes narrowing when he saw Opal snuggled up next to Eli.

Opal slipped out from under his arm and pressed the remote to turn the TV on. "Are you going to watch with us, Myles?"

"No, I just came down to get a drink. I have more computer stuff to do."

Opal thrust out her bottom lip, making Eli want to tell Myles that he could take some time out of whatever he was doing upstairs to watch the half-hour program with his little sisters. But he decided to save his words for what he wanted to say to Myles later when the girls were in bed. No need to antagonize him now.

"Okay," Eli said when the program ended, "time for bed."

"We could watch another program," Opal said. "Mommy wouldn't know."

"Yes, she would," Rose said. "I'd tell her."

"Tattletale!" Opal unfolded her legs from underneath her and stood in front of him. "Do we have to go to bed? Mommy could be home any minute, and then she could tuck us in."

"If your mother was here, would you be asking to stay up later?"

"No," Rose answered for her sister. "Because if she did, Mom wouldn't let her watch any TV tomorrow."

"I see." He pointed across the room. "Upstairs. I'll be up in five minutes to tuck you in."

"Will you read us a story?"

Rose shook her head at Eli. "Mom only reads her a story if she goes to bed early. Come on, Opal, before Mr. Payton gets mad because you're bugging him too much."

Opal looked up at him. "Are you mad at me?"

"No." She was such a cute little imp. He'd have a tough time getting mad or staying mad at her, even if he had a good reason to. "But it is time for you to go to bed."

Five minutes later, Eli went upstairs and almost collided with Myles in the hall outside of the girls' room.

"I'm making sure the girls are in bed," Myles said, with the clear meaning that Eli didn't have to. He stepped in front of Eli and walked into the room.

"It's okay," Opal said as if she were the one in charge. "Myles is a better tucker-inner than he is a cook."

Eli remembered Opal complaining about Myles's cooking the night he'd taken Jamie out to the diner.

"But you can tuck me in, too."

He lifted his foot to step into the room and stopped. "I think Myles can handle it. Good night, Opal, Rose."

"Good night," they chorused.

"When you're done, Myles, please come downstairs. I'd like to talk with you."

"Yeah," Myles said without turning around.

Eli flexed his tight shoulder muscles as he descended the stairs to the living room. Maybe he should leave well enough alone. As Myles had told him, he certainly wasn't the teen's father, wasn't really anything to him, except his guidance counselor. And his mother's friend.

Myles clambered down the stairs. "You said you wanted to talk to me."

"Yeah, sit."

Myles took the recliner and Eli sat on the couch. "I want to clear the air between us."

Myles leaned back in the chair and crossed his arms.

"You don't like it that I'm seeing your mother. That's your prerogative. But the choice as to whether your mother and I see each other is hers and mine, not yours." Or Opal's. Eli's thoughts drifted back to earlier in the evening.

Myles glared at him.

"I'm not your father."

"You've got that right."

"Nor am I trying to be. And you've told me that you're not me. That couldn't be truer. But we do have some things in common."

"Like what?"

"My father was killed in a trucking accident when I was your age."

Myles shrugged.

"It was hard. But I was used to taking care of certain things for Mom because Dad was away making long-distance hauls so often. My mother isn't as handy as yours, so I was responsible for repairs and stuff around the house. After Dad died, I was really protective of Mom. You wouldn't believe what I did to the first guy she dated."

Myles unfolded his arms. "Try me."

"Mom was fixing the guy dinner at our house. My sister was at a friend's house, and I was going to ride my bike down to the lake and meet up with a couple of my friends. I certainly didn't want to stick around and have dinner with them."

That got a half smile out of Myles.

"The guy got there before I left. Mom was upstairs getting ready, so I had to let him in. He'd gone all out with candy and roses. I told him I'd get a vase for the flowers and had him follow me into the dining room, where Mom had the table set with her best dishes and Grandma's silver." Funny how he could picture that table perfectly.

"I went in the kitchen, took out the kitchen shears and snipped off all of the roses into the garbage. Then I filled the vase with water, stuck the flowerless stems in and came back into the dining room. I put the vase in the center of the table, smiled at the guy and called up to Mom that I was leaving, grabbing the candy as I left."

"Get out. You didn't."

"Sadly, I did."

"It got rid of the guy."

"Sure did. It turned out that the guy wasn't keen on kids to begin with, and I validated all of his misgivings about them."

"Did your mom yell at you?"

"Worse. She grounded me for a month and signed me up for group counseling."

"Rough." Myles pushed out of the chair, obviously anxious to make his escape. "I got to go finish my homework."

"But first, we're straight."

"Yeah, it's Mom's choice if she wants to go out with you and I have to be nice to her about it whether I like it or not."

That wasn't exactly what he'd said, but it was good enough for Eli.

"You want to come up and see where you're sleeping? I hope you don't snore."

"I went through twenty years of maneuvers with no complaints. But if you get me a blanket, I'll sack out on the couch, in case your mother gets home sooner than she expected."

"Sure, I'll toss you one down from the closet upstairs."

Eli caught the blanket, folded it over his arm and went into the dining room to turn off the light Rose had left on. Before he flicked the switch, his gaze went to the photo on the wall of Jamie and John. The shadow of the man that seemed to have hung over the house all evening had dissipated.

He stared into his comrade-in-arms's fixed eyes. "I'll take care of her, all of them, for you. If she'll let me."

Chapter Fourteen

Jamie sang out loud as she vacuumed the living room rug. She missed choir. There was no denying it and nothing she could do about it. Nothing, except going back to Hazardtown Community Church. She shoved the couch away from the wall with more effort than necessary and pushed the vacuum back and forth until she was satisfied she'd gotten every bit of dust and dirt up, and had worked away the spark of conflict that had ignited in her about her abandoned faith.

She blamed it on Eli and the easy way he lived his faith, like she once had. At dinner the other evening, it would have been so easy to have bowed her head and joined him in his thanks. But she would have been joining him out of habit, not conviction. Her conviction had died with John. *Or did I simply bury it?*

She turned off the power and heard the vroom

of the school bus pulling away. The kitchen door opened and slammed shut, followed by the sound of boots and other winter gear being shed. She put the vacuum in the hall closet and waited. Opal raced in with Rose a few steps behind her.

"Myles wasn't on the bus," Rose announced.

Jamie closed the closet door. Weariness pressed down on her. Tonight was the first night of bowling league since the alley had reopened after the fire. She hoped Myles's absence wasn't a replay of the other night when he'd "lost track of time" at the garage and she hadn't been able to go to the Career Day committee meeting with Eli. From Myles's attitude lately and from what Eli had said, she'd thought Eli's talk with Myles had diffused a lot of the animosity Myles had for Eli and about them seeing each other.

"Maybe he's getting a ride home with one of his friends," Jamie said. "I bought bananas when I went shopping if you're hungry and want a snack. We're going to have dinner early today because I have bowling."

"Is Autumn coming?" Opal asked.

"No, Myles is going to watch you."

"He'd better get home, then," Rose said.

Exactly what Jamie was thinking. Eli's ringtone chimed on her cell phone. She walked over to the table to pick it up.

"Maybe that's him," Rose said.

"No, that's Mr. Payton. That song always plays when he calls." Opal crossed her arms, obviously pleased that she knew something her older sister didn't.

Jamie didn't even want to contemplate how Opal had figured that out. "Hi," she said into the phone.

"See?" Opal pointed at her. "She's using her nice voice like she always does when she talks to Mr. Payton."

Jamie moved into the hallway, hoping the girls would go get their snack in the kitchen. Did she really use a different voice when she talked with Eli?

"You still there?" Eli asked.

"I was escaping Opal."

"Good luck with that."

She laughed.

"I have Myles here with me."

Jamie's stomach sank. What had he done now?

"Liam's car wouldn't start, and Myles said he'd take a look. Liam had said he'd drive Myles home if he got the car running, but Myles couldn't and he missed the bus. Turned out the battery is dead. We tried jumping it, but no luck."

Jamie leaned against the wall listening to the rhythm of Eli's voice.

"I'm going to drop Liam off at Patrick's. Then, if it's okay with you, I'll swing by my place and change. Myles and I can pick up subs for everyone at the General Store. He says he knows what you all like. You won't have to cook, and we won't be late for bowling."

"We certainly wouldn't want to be late for bowling. Should I expect you here at seventeen hundred hours?"

"Affirmative."

"See you then." Jamie closed her eyes and leaned her head back against the wall.

"Mommy, are you sleeping?" Opal stood at the head of the hallway.

"Of course I'm not sleeping." She hadn't felt this awake and alive in a good long time.

Eli walked Jamie from the bowling alley to his truck. "I think tonight went pretty well."

"You would. You beat me and almost everyone else in the place all three games."

He opened the door for her. "There is that. But I meant getting the subs, dinner with Myles and the girls, and things in general." He closed the door and walked around to his side of the truck. This wasn't the smooth, cool segue he practiced.

"Yes, I think Myles is finally warming to you," she said as he climbed in and shut the door.

But was Myles's mother warming to him? That was the question Eli wanted answered. "The Singles Plus and the youth group at church are sponsoring a concert by Resurrection Light a week from next Thursday during school break. They're a Christian country band from Glens Falls who are making a name for themselves on the national country scene."

"I've seen the signs—everywhere. And I've heard them on Sound of Life. They're good."

"I like them, too." *Lame, Payton, lame.*

Jamie's eyes lit. "Did Myles enlist you to talk up the concert to me so I'll say yes when he asks to go?"

She was still on Myles. "No, I'm talking up the concert so that when I ask you to go with me, you'll say yes."

Jamie opened her mouth.

"You don't have to give me an answer right now. With the concert being at church and the type of music the band plays, I realize you may want to think about it." Although, the fact that Jamie tuned into Sound of Life was a sign in his favor. A sign that, whether she realized it or not, she was open to letting The Lord back into her heart.

"Yes," she said.

His heart pounded. She hadn't hesitated at all.

"I'd like to think about it and let you know. Do you need to buy the tickets in advance?"

The pounding slowed. "They're going to sell fast. I'll go ahead and buy two to make sure we get seats."

"I'll let you know as soon as I decide, so you can line up someone else for the second ticket if I can't go."

"If I don't have anyone to use the second one, the cost will go as an additional contribution to the church. No big deal."

She nodded. "Of course, I'll need to line up a babysitter for Rose and Opal if Myles will be going, which I know he'll want to."

She made it sound like it was almost a done deal. "Anne and Neal and Emily and Drew are going. Neal's folks are watching the kids. They'd probably watch Rose and Opal, too."

Jamie pressed her lips together and furrowed her brow.

He was pushing too hard. Much as he wished it different, he understood that she might be uncomfortable going to a function at church. Lately, he'd been praying that Jamie would see her way back to the fellowship that Community Church had to give her.

"I'll let you know by next Friday."

"Great." He leaned back in the seat and stifled an impulse to whistle one of Resurrection Light's songs.

Over the next few days, Eli's invitation was never far from her mind, especially last Sunday when she'd driven Myles to confirmation class. She'd dropped him at the door. Several people she'd been close with at church waved as they made their way in for adult Sunday school. The waves triggered the vacant feeling she'd had the other Sundays she'd dropped Myles off for his class. If she came to the concert with Eli, would the void fill or would it grow larger?

Jamie cleared the thoughts of church and the concert from her mind as best she could. She had other things to think about right now, namely Career Day. She had to be at the school to set up in twenty minutes. The positive response Becca had gotten from the Scouts, 4-H and other local youth organizations about participating in Career Day had neutralized much of Jamie's opposition to the American Legion youth activities being represented.

When Jamie entered the school, she headed right for the main office to sign in.

"Hi. You're here for Career Day, right?" Thelma Woods motioned Jamie to the sign-in clipboard. "Mr. Payton has sure put together a good program this year."

Jamie signed in and tried not to be irritated by Thelma's use of the formal Mr. Payton, when they both called him Eli, not to mention her discounting Becca's part as committee chairperson in organizing the program and everyone else's work. Jamie picked up the box of literature about the Medical Center that she'd placed on the counter. But that was Thelma's way, and Jamie couldn't argue with her admiration of Eli. Jamie was becoming a fan herself.

Stopping in the doorway to the gym, Jamie glanced around at the people setting up booths. Becca waved to her from the middle of the room. "You're over here," she called.

Jamie lugged her box over. "Looks good." She swept her arm around the room at the tables with their attractive banners, halting at the Armed Forces table where Eli was talking with the uniformed representatives. The animation on his face and in his motions spoke to his belief in the opportunities he thought the service offered. The same belief John had had and she'd once supported.

"Eli's certainly in his element," Becca said.

"Yes, he is." Jamie bit her lip, remembering Myles's threat a few weeks ago to enlist as soon he graduated. If only she could do something to prevent Eli's improved relationship with Myles from unknowingly drawing her son into that element. "I'd better set up. Autumn should be here anytime. She's bringing some educational posters and models and information we have at the office, along with a presentation on her laptop that we put together."

"Sounds good. Anything that gets the kids' attention."

"And I hope it's okay that Autumn talked one of the emergency medical technicians into stopping by later this morning for a while."

"That's great," Becca said. "There's Anne and Neal. I need to show them where to set up."

Jamie turned and waved to her friend and her friend's husband.

"Need any help?" Eli had slipped over beside her while she was waving hello to Anne and Neal.

"Hi, you startled me. All I need to do is put out this literature." She touched the box on the table. "Autumn is bringing the rest of our stuff."

"Then we should make quick work of it. I have some people I'd like to introduce you to."

Jamie dropped her hand to her side. The recruiters. "I don't…" The eager look on Eli's face halted her rebuff. The recruiters were his people. She relented. "Sure."

They quickly organized the table and Eli walked her to the Armed Forces display. "Jamie, this is Lieutenant Second Class Rodney Smith." He introduced her to the Navy representative. "Staff Sergeant Meghan Harrison. And Master Sergeant Jeffrey Kraus from my Air Guard base. Jamie Glasser."

"Ma'am." Lieutenant Smith nodded. "The Lieutenant Colonel told us about your husband. Our condolences."

"We've lost a lot of good people over there," Sergeant Harrison added. Master Sergeant Kraus nodded in agreement.

"Thank you." Jamie braced for the stab of pain that had followed any sympathy offered by her friends and coworkers. She felt a pang of sadness, but no stab. Maybe she was finally moving on as so many people had told her would happen, though she'd refused to believe them.

"Ma'am," Sergeant Harrison said. "The Lieutenant Colonel said you're a nurse. Did you serve?"

"No, I manned the home front. We—I have three children."

"You'll probably meet her son here later," Eli said.

"He's planning to follow in his father's footsteps?" Lieutenant Smith asked.

The man's question brought the stab she hadn't felt earlier. "I hope not. Now, if you'll excuse me, I need to get back and help my colleague finish setting up our booth." She spun around and strode back toward the Medical Center display table.

Eli caught up with her halfway there.

"Jamie." He touched her shoulder.

"Why?" The word was barely more than a whisper.

"Because I'm an idiot? They're comrades. I wanted them to meet you. The mention of Myles just came out." He breathed in and released the breath through his nose. "I seem to have a talent for saying the wrong things around you."

Through the red haze of her pain, Jamie could see that Eli's words were an admission for him, that on some level she rattled the seemingly unshakable Lieutenant Colonel. "Yes, you are good at it. Possibly the best I've seen."

"I could attempt to be worse at it."

"That might be a worthwhile endeavor."

"I'll stop by later and put my efforts to the test." With that, Eli walked away toward Anne and Neal's display.

"What went on there?" Autumn asked when Jamie reached their table.

"Eli put his foot in his mouth again."

"Men have a way of doing that. My dad is an expert. Ask Anne."

"She's told me." Jamie recalled some of the insensitive statements Neal had made during his and Anne's courtship. Eli's weren't any worse.

Five hours later, the last of the students filed out of the gym. As Jamie and Autumn took down their display, Jamie looked around for Eli. She'd half expected, no, hoped he'd stop by at lunchtime to join her and Anne and Neal, but he hadn't. She didn't see him in the gym now, either.

"That does it," Autumn said, closing her laptop. "I think it was a pretty successful day, don't you?"

"Hmm?" Jamie focused on what she thought Autumn had said. "Some of the kids seemed really interested in medical careers and asked good questions. Others, not so much, like the three girls who were seeing who could pick up information from each of the displays first."

"Yes," Autumn agreed, "one of them got hung up

at the recruiters' booth. Can't blame her. The Navy guy is kind of cute, although far too old for her."

Jamie looked over at the table where the recruiters were taking down their display. "Second Lieutenant Rodney Smith." She gave the man a fast once-over. He was sort of attractive. She hadn't noticed when Eli had introduced them.

"You know him? I saw you and Eli talking with him when I came in."

"Eli introduced us."

"Want to introduce me?" Autumn grinned. "There aren't many new men around here for me to meet."

After the abrupt ending she'd put to her earlier conversation with the man, Jamie wasn't sure she wanted to face him again.

"Jamie. I'm glad I caught you." Becca approached her and Autumn. "Eli would like you to wait for him."

Jamie ignored Autumn's raised eyebrow.

"He got delayed in a meeting with the parents of one of my homeroom students."

"I suppose I can. I'll have to text Myles and let him know I may get home after he and the girls do." Jamie texted him and got an immediate "K."

"He said he'd be down as soon as he finishes. Or now," Becca said when Eli appeared in the doorway. "I've got to run. Brendon's kindergarten teacher is keeping him and I don't want to hold her up."

"See you. Do you still want that introduction?" Jamie asked Autumn. "I'm sure Eli would be glad to."

"Did I hear my name?" Eli smiled at her and then over at Autumn as if as an afterthought.

"Yes, I told Autumn you'd be happy to introduce her to Lieutenant Smith."

"No." Autumn waved them off. "I think I'll go introduce myself and leave you to do whatever you have planned."

"We don't have anything—" Autumn stopped Jamie with a pointed look at Eli.

"Mention your dad," Eli said. "I think Rodney knows him from the American Legion."

Autumn gave him a thumbs-up and made a bee-line for the recruiter table.

Eli sat on the edge of the table. "So, how do you think it went?"

"Good." He'd wanted her to stay to make small talk?

"If you're free, I thought we could stop and have coffee before you have to get home. When I talked with Myles earlier, he was good with watching Rose and Opal."

No wonder Myles was so agreeable when she'd texted him. She put her hands on her hips and attempted a stern look. "You guys set me up."

"Yes, we did." He pushed off the table and picked

up the box she'd packed. "Now, get a move on it. I've only bought his time for an hour and a half."

"You paid Myles?"

"I told him I'd order his favorite pizza for you to bring home with you. He said no one likes his cooking."

"More like Opal The Vocal doesn't like his cooking. I assume you're joining us for pizza." Apparently, he had her whole evening planned. Not that she minded.

"No, sorry. Mom called and asked me to stop by and reprogram her DVR on my way to the Singles Plus meeting. I'm in charge tonight, so I have to be there. I'm sure Mom will have made dinner for me."

"Oh, okay." A feeling of disappointment and longing tugged at her. She certainly wouldn't mind spending the evening with Eli, and she used to really enjoy the Singles Plus group.

Eli helped her finish packing up the display and carried her things out to her car. She followed him in her car to the pizzeria. Eli ordered the pizza, and they took their coffee to a table in the back away from the busy takeout counter to wait out the half hour the person who took his order said it would take to be ready.

Jamie peered at him over her mug. "Can I ask you a question about Myles?"

Eli placed his coffee on the table and wrapped his hands around the mug. "Sure."

"Has he ever said anything to you, as his guidance counselor, about a medical career?"

"No, why?"

"I expected him to stay glued to the recruiters' display the whole time his class was in the gym. He stopped by it but spent most of his time talking to the emergency medical technician Autumn lined up to join us. The EMT told me Myles took a brochure on EMT and paramedic training. Now that's a uniform I could breathe easier seeing him wear."

Eli picked up his mug and took a long draw of coffee. "You can only protect him so much. He's going to grow up and make his own choices."

Jamie sighed. "I know. Just as long as he doesn't do it too fast, so I have time to guide him toward making the right choices." *And not some of the choices his father and I made,* she added to herself.

"He'll do okay," Eli reassured her. "Myles has a good head on his shoulders when he chooses to use it. You've done a good job with him, and Rose and Opal, too."

"Thanks. It hasn't always been easy."

"I don't think parenting ever is. And you've done most of it alone."

Jamie worked a muscle in her jaw.

"I don't mean any offense. Military families have special challenges, with the potential for one or both parents to be deployed at any time."

"We thought we knew what we were getting

into. But we were so young, and Myles came along sooner than we'd planned. John was away so much." *And then he was gone.*

Eli nodded. "I saw the stress some of my married friends and their families were under. I decided early in my career that I wouldn't put a kid through that, wouldn't have children while I was in the service." His voice dropped. "My fiancée disagreed."

Jamie sympathized with him, but she disagreed, too. "I wouldn't give up having my kids for anything. They're all I have now of John."

Eli's lips curved into a sad smile.

She hadn't meant to sound maudlin or have Eli feel sorry for her. It was simply a fact of her life. "Speaking of my kids, I'd better get home to them while the house is still standing." Jamie looked up at the clock on the wall. "With my twenty-minute drive, I should make it home in just under your paid-for time. I'd hate to be responsible for Myles charging you time-and-a-half overtime." Jamie's attempt to put a lighter tone on the conversation fell flat.

"I'll get the pizza." He settled up and walked her to her car.

Jamie unlocked the door and got in. He handed her the pizza, resting his hand on the top corner of the door while she placed the box on the passenger seat. He was still holding the door when she reached to pull it shut.

"Have you decided?" He shifted his weight from one foot to the other. "About the concert?"

His hesitation made him appear almost boyish. She looked up at the figure looming beside her vehicle. But Eli Payton was all man. A man who appealed to her in so many ways—his strength, his way with her kids, his generosity. Still, her feelings about the military were at odds with his. Even though he was retired from active duty, it remained a part of his life through his involvement with the Air Guard and the American Legion. And she couldn't see Eli being happy with a woman who didn't share his strong faith, especially one who once had. She'd be wise to cool their friendship now while she was still thinking with her head and not her heart.

He leaned in the car and brushed his lips against hers. "I don't have to know right now," he said, his breath warm against her cheek.

Almost before his action could register in her mind, he straightened and smiled down at her.

Her heart took over. "Yes, I'd like to go to the concert."

Chapter Fifteen

The rap on the front door reverberated up the stairs to Jamie's room.

He can't be here already. She hadn't even done her makeup yet. Jamie checked her alarm clock. Eli was a full fifteen minutes early. She should have expected it. But it had been so nice to have the house all to herself that she'd dawdled in her bath. Anne's mother-in-law, Mary, who was watching Rose and Opal tonight, had taken the girls early to give Jamie time to get ready, and Myles had gone over to Tanner's this afternoon.

The rap sounded again. She glanced in the mirror at the soft ivory silk blouse she wore over the dressy jeans she'd bought last weekend because she really needed a new pair, not because of the concert. Except for a lack of jewelry, she looked fairly together. She hurried to the door before Eli could knock again.

Jamie opened the door and a look of surprise crossed Eli's face. He'd probably expected to see Opal since she was his usual greeter. "Hi, come in. You're a little early."

He checked his watch.

Why had she said that?

Eli ran his gaze over her. "You look nice."

"Thanks." She warmed. It had been a while since anyone other than Rose or Opal had commented on her appearance.

He glanced around. "No kids?"

"No, they're all at their designated posts for the night. I'm almost ready. Give me five."

"I'm not going anywhere without you."

Her heart skittered. What was with her? She and Eli had gone out before. At this rate, she was going to be total mush by the time they got to the concert. Standing in front of the mirror in the upstairs bath, she breathed deeply to steady her hand so she could apply her makeup. She finished and, after a final check in the mirror, closed her makeup case. In her room, she added the turquoise pendant and matching earrings she'd bought when she'd picked up the new jeans.

"All set." She smiled at Eli as she descended the stairs. Even though they were now running a little late, he took what seemed to her an extraordinarily long time helping her on with her coat. And she didn't mind one bit.

* * *

Eli pulled open the door to the church hall, his gaze on Jamie alert to any hesitation she might show. On the drive to her house, he'd gone back and forth over whether he'd made a good move inviting her to the concert. Much as he tried to tell himself that he'd invited her for the music, deep down he knew he also hoped it might be an opening for Jamie to return to God and Hazardtown Community Church. Lately, he'd sensed that she wasn't as far from her previous relationship with God as he'd previously thought.

"Looks like a good turnout," Jamie said as he took her coat and handed it to a teen from his youth group who was volunteering as a coat-check person.

"Yeah, it sold out fast. I would have had no problem finding someone to take your ticket if you'd decided not to come."

"Well, don't think you're going to get rid of me now."

"Not a chance." He placed his hand on the small of her back. "There's Neal and Anne. I thought we'd sit with them."

"Good."

He walked her to the seats their friends had saved for them, pleased to have the most beautiful woman in the room beside him.

"Hi," Anne said. "I'm so glad you came. Have you heard Resurrection Light before?"

"A few times on the radio. Myles likes them."

"I've become a big fan. The lead singer is from Ticonderoga, and I heard that because we're a home-town audience, they may sing a new song that's not going to be released until next week."

Eli waited for Jamie to sit and then made himself comfortable in the chair next to her, resting his arm on the back of her seat. As the band worked through its set, he dropped his arm around her shoulders. The music wound down and the lead singer stepped back to the microphone. "We're going to take a twenty minute break then come back for another set. I hear there are some refreshments to keep you entertained until then."

The dimmed lights turned up and Eli and Jamie rose to walk over to the kitchen side of the hall. He took her hand and she slipped her fingers between his, as if it were a natural thing for her to do.

"Eli." Patrick Russell stopped them halfway there.

"Patrick. I didn't know you were coming."

"Brett got us tickets. I want to thank you again for all the help you've given him with the Air Force Academy application."

"No problem. So he's here with you?" Eli looked past Patrick.

Patrick shook his head. "No," he said in a sub-dued voice. "I'm here with Charlie."

Jamie's hand stiffened in Eli's.

"I want to thank you and the Community Church

prayer chain for that, too. I think your prayers gave me the strength I needed to convince Charlie to get help. We're giving things a second try." Patrick looked over his shoulder. "She'd like to apologize to you for all of the trouble she caused, if you'll let her."

Eli nodded. He had no problem hearing Charlie's apology. Eli could forgive her, even if he might not ever be able to forget all she'd done. He wasn't so sure about Jamie. He squeezed her hand and she squeezed his back.

"She's over by the coat room." Patrick led them to his wife.

"Jamie, Eli. I didn't know if you'd come, and I couldn't blame you if you'd refused." Charlie raised her hand, palm out. "Let me say what I need to say before I lose my nerve. I did some awful things to a lot of people, not the least of which was spreading lies about the two of you. I'm sorry. I'm particularly sorry for hurting Rose. I hurt Katy, too." Charlie's voice caught.

Patrick slipped his arm around his wife's waist. "Without getting into details, there's a medical cause for some of it."

"But not all of it." Charlie stopped her husband's excuses. "I have to take responsibility for my actions." She touched Eli's arm. "I hope that someday you might be able to forgive me for holding my unfounded grudge against you all of these years and refusing to believe what I knew was true about Brett. I hurt him, too, and Patrick more."

Patrick rubbed Charlotte's back.

Eli reached deep inside himself. "I forgive you."

"Thank you." Tears ran down Charlie's face. She turned to Jamie. "I know I have no right to ask anything of you, but I hope you can find it in your heart to not hold the sins of the mother against the child and let Katy and Rose remain friends."

Jamie clutched Eli's hand, and her throat muscles worked to swallow. To Eli, the silence surrounding the four of them seemed interminable.

"I forgive you, for Eli's and the kids' sakes as well as yours." Jamie looked into his eyes, and his heart swelled. "But you'll have to forgive me, too. For the time being, Katy can come to our house, but I can't let Rose come to yours."

"Fair enough. Thanks again to both of you."

"Charlie and I are seeing Pastor Joel for counseling, too," Patrick added.

"He's very good," Jamie said in a voice barely above a whisper.

Sounds of the band tuning up punctuated her statement.

"We'd better get back to our seats," Patrick said. "We'll see you Sunday, Eli."

Jamie was quiet on the walk back to their seats. Eli wanted to tell her he was proud of her for accepting Charlie's apology and acknowledging

Pastor Joel's power as a counselor. His mother had told him Jamie wouldn't accept Joel's help after her husband had been killed. But Eli couldn't put the right words together and didn't want to chance his admiration coming out wrong.

"I thought you'd gotten lost." Neal hailed them as they approached their seats.

"Lost? Never. We took a short detour." Eli would let his friend weigh that one.

The band ran through its second set. "Now we have something special for you," the lead singer said.

"I was right," Anne said. "They *are* going to play their new song."

"Who would have thought my engineering professor wife would become a country-band groupie," Neal said.

"I am not." Anne slapped his arm. "I simply like them."

"It's okay. Tonight has made me as big a fan as you are. I'm glad I came," Jamie said.

"I'm glad you did, too," Eli said for her ears only.

The band's lead singer moved front and center. "The next song is from our new album that's releasing next week. It's a tribute to all of our men and women in uniform and all that they and their families give up for us."

The crowd responded with thundering applause. As the song moved from the first verse to the refrain, "Don't worry about me when I'm gone. My memories of you will bring me home," Jamie's shoulders tensed under Eli's arm. This wasn't the follow-up she needed to Charlie's apology. After a moment, she relaxed and continued to tap her foot to the music as she had all evening, except with less enthusiasm. Or did he only imagine less enthusiasm?

The start of the final verse brought a quiet gasp from her.

"Do you want to leave?"

She shook her head.

As the band rolled into the final refrain, tears fell freely down her face. "Don't worry about me. I'll be thinking of you when I go home to Jesus... I'll be praying for your hurt to go away when I'm on my way to Jesus... Don't worry about me. I'll be rooting for you to go on with your life when I'm at home with Jesus."

Eli stared at her helplessly. What had he done? Tonight was supposed to have been a fun night out for Jamie. And it was turning out to be anything but.

At the end of the song, Jamie stood with the others in clapping an ovation, tears streaking her cheeks. Eli mechanically brought his hands together while his mind rolled over ways to try to make things up to Jamie.

Eli was surprised at the way Jamie held herself together saying goodbye to Anne and Neal and other people they saw walking out of the hall. Her determination to be strong made his heart ache. He so wanted to take some of the pain for her but didn't know how to.

"I'm sorry," he said as he unlocked the passenger side door of his truck.

Her head jerked up, almost as if she had just noticed him there with her. "John would have liked you. A lot."

Somehow, her random statement seemed totally appropriate. "I'm sure I would have liked him, too." He pulled the door open for her. How could he not like someone Jamie had loved?

Jamie lapsed back into her contemplative silence for the short drive to her house.

"I'm happy you asked me to come tonight," she said as he pulled into her driveway.

"Despite Charlie and the last song?"

"No, more because of Charlie and the last song. They made me see some things more clearly that I didn't want to see before."

"And that's good?"

"That's good."

At the front door, she tilted her face to him and he reached for her. A light went on in her neighbor's house and he stopped.

"It's okay," she said. "I don't care who sees us."

He drew her into his arms and kissed her with a tenderness fueled by the uncertainty that had plagued him all evening, and she returned the kiss with a fierceness that reignited his desire to protect her from all the harms and hurts of the world.

Chapter Sixteen

Jamie kept an ear tuned to the radio for a weather update as she cleaned up after lunch. The weather report she'd seen on the morning news had forecast a possible nor'easter that could drop as much as three feet of snow this evening and overnight or, if the storm stalled, late tonight and tomorrow morning. The meteorologist on the radio wasn't any more specific.

"Mom, do you know where my green long-sleeved T-shirt is?"

"I would guess in your dirty clothes hamper or clean clothes basket, depending on whether or not you did your laundry."

"You're not any help." Myles rushed back out of the room.

Jamie wouldn't have let him get away with that, except she suspected her baby boy was in puppy love. The church youth group was going to a Bible trivia competition in Glens Falls this afternoon. Normally, Myles wouldn't give a thought to what he was wearing. That is, before the new girl at school joined the youth group. She smiled, letting the cute factor block out her concern about the weather.

"I found it," Myles shouted from the other room.

"Good," she shouted back, glancing out the window at Rose and Opal building a snow fort in the back yard. A snowball arced from the corner of the house and fell in the center of the square the girls were walling in. They both threw snowballs back at the tall figure that came around the corner. Jamie's heart thrummed.

"Mr. Payton is here," Opal said as she burst inside.

"So, I see."

Eli grinned at her.

She wiped her hands and walked to the door. "But how did he get all covered in snow?"

"We threw snowballs at him."

"He started it," Rose said, laughing.

"Guilty as charged." He leaned forward as if to kiss her hello, then straightened when Opal reminded him to wipe his feet.

"We're going to go back out and finish our fort," Rose said, and she and Opal trooped out.

The door firmly closed, Eli gave her a quick peck. "Hi."

"Hi. Myles is almost ready."

Eli looked at the kitchen clock. "Yes, I'm early."

"I've been keeping track of the weather."

Eli pulled off his gloves. "Yeah, so have Pastor Joel and I, and he's talked with some of the parents. They all seemed to think it was just weather as usual. Besides, the report I saw on the Weather Channel right before I left said the storm is slowing and may not even reach this far north."

"That would be fine with me."

"Me, too." He placed his gloves on the counter and took her hands. "I'll take care of him. I might not have grown up in the Buffalo Snowbelt, but I've done my share of winter driving here in the mountains."

"I know." She shrugged. "But I worry anyway."

"You're a mother. Pastor and I talked it over. We don't expect any problems." Or at least he'd convinced Pastor the weather wasn't problematic. The kids were really up for the competition, and the weather reporters were yet to be right about a single big storm they'd forecast this winter. "You know we wouldn't put the kids in danger."

Myles bounded into the kitchen. "I'm ready."

"Let's go. We'll see you around eight," Eli said.

From the window in the door, she watched them tromp through the snow and around the house to the driveway. John's last words to her echoed in her head. *"I'll see you June 28."* She shook them away. Eli and Myles weren't marching off to war.

They were going to Prince of Peace Church in Glens Falls, an hour away. The sun broke through the clouds and shone brilliantly on the snow-covered yard. They'd be fine.

Eli leaned forward, keeping an iron grip on the church van steering wheel, trying to see better out of the small window of vision in the windshield. The wipers and defroster were fighting a tough battle with the blinding wet snow. Behind him, the kids chatted and joked, seemingly oblivious to the storm. They trusted him, as Jamie trusted him to bring Myles home. Eli glimpsed a familiar landmark. *Only seven miles to go.* As he inched around the curve, he felt the fifteen-seat van lose traction with the snow-covered pavement. He fought the skid, but no matter what he tried, the van continued heading toward the guardrail. The helplessness of not having any control made him sick to his stomach.

"Please, Lord, let the guardrail stop us." He didn't know if he spoke out loud or to himself. It didn't matter. He didn't want to think of what could happen if they went through the guardrail and down the mountainside.

One of the girls screamed, and they all seemed to join her in a deafening roar as the van hit the guardrail, flipped over and rolled down into the ravine, the sound of crunching metal vying with the noise from the kids.

"Lord, please," he roared over the din. In answer, the van stopped upright against some pine trees. From what Eli could see out of his side window, they weren't too far down the mountain.

He shut the engine off, released his seat belt and rubbed his shoulder where the belt had restrained him. He rose and the van rocked. How long would the trees hold? Between the trunks, Eli saw the wide expanse of white sloping down to the bottom of the ravine far below. The wind howled and swayed the trees, but the van didn't move any more. They were big old trees with deep roots. They should hold if no one made any sudden moves.

"Is everyone okay?"

He received a few weak responses of "Yeah" and "I think so." A powerful, guilt-laced relief shot through him when he heard Myles's voice among them.

"My leg hurts really bad." Tanner's voice held a quiver that he was obviously trying to hide.

"And my head is bleeding," Sara shrieked.

Eli removed the first aid kit from the van glove compartment. He went to Sara first. Fortunately, her cut wasn't deep. He bandaged it. "You're okay. Head wounds always seem worse because they bleed more. Hold your hand against the bandage. The pressure will help stop the bleeding."

He moved down the aisle to check Tanner's leg. "It looks like it's broken." He wasn't a medic, but he'd seen enough broken bones in his time. "Keep it as still as you can."

Tanner nodded.

"Mr. Payton," a teary voice called from the far back before he could say more. "It's Seth." Ava, Seth's girlfriend, who'd joined the group after the sledding party, sobbed. "He's not moving."

Eli moved to the back as fast as he could without causing any undue motion. He broke open smelling salts and waved the capsule under Seth's nose in hopes that he might have fainted, but he got no reaction from the teen.

"Is he…?" Ava's voice rose to a high-pitched screech.

"He probably has a concussion." Eli had trouble not being short with the girl's near hysterics. He was as on edge as they were but couldn't risk showing it. "Everyone stay calm." He turned to Myles in the opposite seat. "I'm going to hand you some blankets." Eli pulled a pile of blankets from a compartment behind the last seat and gave them to Myles. "Walk up to the front very carefully and pass them out to the other kids. Depending on how long it takes help to get here, we might need them later to keep warm."

"Okay." Jamie's coffee-brown eyes stared back at him from the youth's serious face. He *had* to get them all out of here safely. He had no other recourse.

Eli placed a blanket over Seth and handed the rest to Myles.

"Why can't you turn the van back on and run the heat to keep us warm?" one of the girls asked.

"Duh," one of the guys said. "Like, if the gas tank is damaged, we could be toast."

"Quiet!" Just what he didn't need: someone getting the kids more panicked. Eli walked up to the front of the van where Myles stood, handing out the last of the blankets. The teen's expression reflected a confidence in Eli that he was hard-pressed to match.

"I'm going to call for help." He took his phone from his pocket. *No reception.* He punched in Pastor's number anyway, but it didn't ring. "I didn't get through." He had to be up-front with the kids. "Everyone stay still while I try to open the door."

If he got up to the road, maybe he could get a connection. He pulled the handle and pushed the door. It squeaked open a half inch and stopped. The van must have hit a boulder or something on the way down that dented the side and jammed the door. Squinting into the blinding snow pummeling the window, he pressed his shoulder and all of his weight against the door. The van swayed and a couple of the kids yelped.

Panic choked him. His insistence that the weather wouldn't be a problem had put the kids in danger. How would he face Jamie and ever forgive himself if Myles was hurt? She'd become his heart. The van rocked again. What if he never saw her again? He glimpsed the desolation Jamie must have experienced when she lost her husband and had an inkling of how that had tested her faith. Then, his years of readiness training kicked back in.

"Here's what we're going to do. Pastor Joel was behind us. I'm sure he stopped."

Eli wasn't sure at all. If Joel hadn't been right behind them and seen them go over, in this snow, he'd have no clue they were here.

"I'm going to open the window, and on the count of three, you're going to all shout 'help' three times, then stop and listen for a response." He turned the van on accessory and hit the window button. It rolled halfway down. *Good enough.* "Okay. Ready? One, two…" Eli felt Myles and the other kids behind them almost vibrating, waiting for him to say three.

"Three."

"Help, help, help." Their united voices reverberated in the van and echoed up the ravine.

Lord, please have someone hear us. It was out of his hands now.

They heard nothing in return but the wind in the trees and the silence of the winter night.

Jamie had tucked the girls in bed at nine, despite their protests that tomorrow wasn't a school day. Now that they were settled down, she flicked through the channels on the TV while the storm winds howled outside. *Eli had said they'd be home by eight.*

The ring of the house phone made her jump. "Hello."

"Jamie, it's Anne."

Something in Anne's voice set her heart racing.

"We think the church van may have gone off the road on the way back from Glens Falls."

"What do you mean, you think?" Jamie shouted.

Anne ignored her friend's panic. "Pastor Joel was following the van. Visibility is really poor. He thought the van was right ahead of him. Joel got to the church a few minutes ago, expecting to see Eli and the other kids there. They weren't."

Anne's words pressed all of the air out of Jamie's lungs. "Myles?"

"Is in the van."

"No!"

"Pastor Joel called 911, and he and Neal just left to retrace the route back to the last spot Pastor saw the van. The other parents are here at the church. They were waiting to pick their kids up. Jennifer has organized a prayer vigil while she waits for word from her husband and Neal. If you'd like to join them, I'll come over and stay with Rose and Opal. My kids are with Neal's parents."

"Why would I want to do that? What good will it do?"

A moment of silence answered her. "I can come over anyway, so you don't have to wait alone."

Fatigue overwhelmed her, making the phone receiver feel like a lead weight in her hand. "No, I'll be all right. Call me as soon as you have news." She clicked off and heaved the phone at the opposite end of the couch. "No, not again. Not Myles. Eli said he'd bring him home." *Eli.* Grief for what she feared most—the loss of him and Myles—seared her, and she dissolved in tears.

A voice from the past, the voice of the chaplain at Fort Drum, broke through the red haze. *So be strong and courageous! Do not be afraid and do not panic before them. For the Lord your God will personally go ahead of you. He will neither fail you nor abandon you.* Deuteronomy 31:6. The chaplain had been reassuring the wife of a newly deployed recruit at their spousal Bible study.

She could see Eli embracing these words, as she once had. He had as perfect a faith as she'd ever seen. He'd spoken his heart when he'd said they'd be home. She longed to give her fears to a higher power, to lean on one stronger than her. She realized that Eli had tried to give her some of that strength. But he'd be the first to say that any strength he had to give came from above. Could she draw on that strength? Did she still have it in her? Or had her bitterness killed all of her faith, as she'd let herself believe?

Sinking to her knees, she prayed, "Dear Lord,

even if only for tonight, allow me back into Your flock so that I might see my way again. And, even though I'm unworthy to ask anything of You, I know You'll hear my prayer for Eli and Myles and the other kids to be safe tonight."

A knock at the door brought Jamie to her feet. She looked out to see Anne and opened the door.

"I couldn't leave you alone," Anne said.

"Come in." Jamie closed the door and took Anne's coat. Her friend's kindness in coming even though Jamie had rebuffed her earlier offer threatened to trigger another torrent of tears. "If you're still willing to stay with the girls, I'd like to go join the other parents at the prayer vigil."

"Oh, Jamie." Anne hugged her. "Of course my offer is still open. The snow has let up a lot, but drive carefully, and God bless."

Jamie hugged her back, fervently hoping for the last.

She walked into the church hall and Tanner's mother, Clare, rushed to her, followed by Patrick and Charlie at a more hesitant gait. Jamie hugged them all.

"Jennifer is waiting to hear from Pastor Joel again," Clare said. "When she talked with him about fifteen minutes ago, he and Neal had found the spot where the van had gone off the road and the mountain rescue team had just arrived."

"So, you haven't heard… You don't know?"

Jamie stumbled putting the words together into a cohesive question.

"Come and join us in the prayer circle," Patrick said.

Clare touched her arm. "You don't have to if it makes you uncomfortable. We understand."

Jamie thought of the numerous invitations to come to service and church functions that Clare had offered over the past months. "I'd like to. Very much."

An aura of hope and peace enclosed her as she took her place in the circle and joined hands with Clare and Charlie. As she prayed with the others, Jamie more fully realized what she already knew in her heart. The military and Eli by association weren't the enemy. As tonight was proving, everyday life could be as dangerous. Nor was trust in others or God or church her enemy. Not trusting in any of them was her scapegoat to allow her not to accept life and live it to the fullest. *Thank You, Lord, for leading me from the wilderness.*

The phone on the wall near the kitchen rang and everyone turned to look at it. Jennifer answered. "Hello. Yes, yes. Praise the Lord." She hung up and turned to the parents. "The rescue squad has them all out. There doesn't seem to be any life-threatening injuries. They're taking them to the Adirondack Medical Center in Saranac Lake to be checked out by the emergency room doctors, though, just to be safe."

"Amen!" one of the fathers said.

The parents made the hour drive to Saranac Lake in a car caravan. Jamie prayed the whole time that the information Jennifer had gotten was right.

Eli spotted Jamie as soon as she walked into the waiting room to await her turn to talk with the doctor. He hung back out of her line of vision. Tonight's experience, more than any he'd had in combat, brought home how precious life was when you loved someone. As he watched Jamie, he longed to take her into his arms and tell her how much he loved her. He couldn't think of anything he'd rather do than spend the rest of his life doing his best to love and protect her and her family.

But he'd failed her. He'd put her son in danger, and he'd put himself in danger. He had no right to insinuate himself in her life. Eli didn't know how Jamie had coped with losing her husband. Before the rescue squad had arrived, when their fate was uncertain, he thought of not seeing her again and the pain was indescribable. He was a fool. He'd thought to give her strength to lean on. She was far stronger than him.

"Ms. Glasser," the nurse called Jamie into the emergency room. A couple of minutes later she emerged, arm around Myles, smiling.

Eli had thought Myles was fine, but it lightened his heart to have that confirmed. He rose to slip out the back door. His apologies would be better made later, in private.

"Where do you think you're going, buster?" Jamie's voice stopped him.

Although he'd rather have her make the break privately, if she needed to do it here, he could take it like a man.

He pasted a smile on his face. "Myles is all right?"

"He's fine." She turned to her son. "Why don't you help Tanner's mother get him to her car? Crutches are tricky until you get the hang of them."

Myles left and Eli had to face Jamie alone.

"Did you really think you were going to sneak out of this hospital without talking to me?"

"That was the idea," he admitted.

She led him to an alcove off the waiting room. "Thank you."

"You're thanking me?"

"I trusted you to bring Myles home safe and you did. Myles told me how you kept everyone calm and under control until the emergency squad got there. How you led them in prayer and made him feel confident he'd get out okay. Then, how you worked right along with the rescuers until everyone was out of the van and up on the road."

"I did what I was able to do. But I didn't do it alone."

"I know. You did it with God's help. I realized

tonight that in order to trust anything, anyone, I have to trust our Lord first."

"Oh, Jamie." He pulled her into his arms. "I love you."

"I love you, too."

He held her close, feeling her heart beat against his chest, and kissed her with every ounce of love he had in him. He lifted his head. "I can't describe the terror I felt when I thought I might not see you again." He took a deep breath. "I want to keep seeing you. I like having you and your family in my life."

Jamie smiled at him, her eyes half-shuttered. "I think that could be arranged." She ran her finger down the side of his chin. "On a couple conditions."

"And what might those conditions be?"

"You don't try to regiment my life and you allow me to be late every now and then."

He rested his hands on her waist. "You're a hard taskmaster, but I'm up to the assignment. Now, I'd better walk you out before Myles starts wondering where we are."

"Let him wonder." She reached up and pulled his head down and kissed him.

Epilogue

Jamie bent her head and breathed the sweet smell of her rose bouquet. *Lord, thank You for Your patience with me and for bringing Eli into my life and me back into Your loving family.*

The organ chord sounded signaling the start of the procession. Anne, her matron of honor, turned and smiled at her as Rose and Opal started down the aisle.

"Mommy!" Opal turned and said in a loud stage whisper that echoed through the church. "When the wedding is over, can I call Mr. Payton Daddy or do I still have to call him Mr. Payton?" Laughter rippled through the church.

"I think he would love for you to call him Daddy," Jamie said. "Now go back up with Rose."

Jamie's father bent down and whispered in her ear. "Eli's a good man. I hope he recognizes all of the treasures he's getting." Her father raised his chin toward Rose and Opal, now halfway down the aisle, and Myles standing at the altar rail.

Her gaze traveled from Myles to Neal to the spot where Eli should be standing. He wasn't there. Why would they have started the procession? Her heart stopped. Eli was never late.

Anne touched her arm. "It's okay. He's here. The guys played a trick on him. Last night at the bachelor party, Pastor Joel got ahold of Eli's watch on some pretext and set it back. And Leah did the same with the clocks at his place."

Jamie's giggle was stopped short by Eli rushing in the side door, resplendent in Air Force dress uniform.

Her gaze locked with his, and the love reflected in his eyes filled her heart to bursting. She walked down the aisle on her father's arm, oblivious to everything but Eli standing military-straight in front of the altar. When she stepped beside Eli, he took her hand in his and squeezed, strong and firm.

"Ready?" Pastor Joel whispered.

Eli dropped his gaze to Jamie's upturned face and gave a decisive nod.

"Yes," she whispered back, holding Eli's gaze. And she was. Ready to give all her love to the man beside her. Ready, with Eli by her side, to face and accept whatever God might have in store for them.

* * * * *

Dear Readers,

Welcome back to Paradox Lake for widow Jamie Glasser's story. If you read *Small-Town Dad*, you'll recall that Jamie was manning the home-front waiting for her husband to return from duty in Afghanistan. He never made it home, and now Jamie has turned away from her faith and anything military. So who does God put in her path at every turn? Retired Air Force Lt. Colonel Eli Payton—youth group leader and Sunday school teacher at Jamie's former church *and* Jamie's troubled son's high school guidance teacher.

The inspiration for *Small-Town Mom* came from a prayer we say at our church every week for our nation's men and women in uniform. Not coming from a military background, it was a challenge to write. I hope you'll find reading it as rewarding as I found writing it.

Please feel free to email me at JeanCGordon@yahoo.com or snail mail me at PO Box 113, Selkirk, NY 12158. You can also visit me at Facebook.com/JeanCGordon.author or JeanCGordon.com or Tweet me at @JeanCGordon.

Blessings,
Jean C. Gordon

Questions for Discussion

1. Have you ever had an event in your life that pushed your faith to its limits?

2. What did you do?

3. Why do you think Jamie was unable to hold on to her faith after her husband was killed?

4. Could Eli have done more to bring Jamie back closer to God? What?

5. If Jamie were your friend, what would you have done to help her?

6. Do you agree or disagree with Jamie's reasoning for allowing her son Myles to attend confirmation classes. Why or why not?

7. How do you think Eli's childhood and military career colored his first impressions of Jamie?

8. Do you think those impressions were justified in any way? Why or why not?

9. Is Eli's military background a positive or negative factor in his working with teenagers at school and church?

10. Do you think Jamie overreacted to Charlotte Russell's behavior toward her and Eli? Why or why not?

11. How well do you think Eli handled the situation? Why?

12. At what point would you have been able to forgive Charlotte?

13. Have you ever had something you'd done when you were younger come back and cause problems later?

14. Do you think Jamie was right in vocalizing her resistance to having representatives of the Armed Forces at Career Day, even though she knew the other committee members would disagree with her?

15. Was Eli out of line talking to Myles about Eli and Jamie's budding relationship without talking with her first?

16. Do you think Jamie would have found her way back to God and Community Church without Eli's example?

LARGER-PRINT BOOKS!

GET 2 FREE
LARGER-PRINT NOVELS
PLUS 2 FREE
MYSTERY GIFTS

Love Inspired®

Larger-print novels are now available...

LILPDIR13R

LARGER-PRINT BOOKS!

GET 2 FREE
LARGER-PRINT NOVELS
PLUS 2 FREE
MYSTERY GIFTS

Love Inspired®
SUSPENSE
RIVETING INSPIRATIONAL ROMANCE

Larger-print novels are now available...

YES! Please send me 2 FREE LARGER-PRINT Love Inspired® Suspense novels and my 2 FREE mystery gifts (gifts are worth about $10). After receiving them, if I don't wish to receive any more books, I can return the shipping statement marked "cancel." If I don't cancel, I will receive 4 brand-new novels every month and be billed just $5.24 per book in the U.S. or $5.74 per book in Canada. That's a savings of at least 23% off the cover price. It's quite a bargain! Shipping and handling is just 50¢ per book in the U.S. and 75¢ per book in Canada.* I understand that accepting the 2 free books and gifts places me under no obligation to buy anything. I can always return a shipment and cancel at any time. Even if I never buy another book, the two free books and gifts are mine to keep forever.

110/310 IDN F5CC

Name _____ (PLEASE PRINT) _____

Address _____ Apt. # _____

City _____ State/Prov. _____ Zip/Postal Code _____

Signature (if under 18, a parent or guardian must sign)

Mail to the **Harlequin® Reader Service:**
IN U.S.A.: P.O. Box 1867, Buffalo, NY 14240-1867
IN CANADA: P.O. Box 609, Fort Erie, Ontario L2A 5X3

**Are you a current subscriber to Love Inspired Suspense books
and want to receive the larger-print edition?
Call 1-800-873-8635 or visit www.ReaderService.com.**

* Terms and prices subject to change without notice. Prices do not include applicable taxes. Sales tax applicable in N.Y. Canadian residents will be charged applicable taxes. Offer not valid in Quebec. This offer is limited to one order per household. Not valid for current subscribers to Love Inspired Suspense larger-print books. All orders subject to credit approval. Credit or debit balances in a customer's account(s) may be offset by any other outstanding balance owed by or to the customer. Please allow 4 to 6 weeks for delivery. Offer available while quantities last.

Your Privacy—The Harlequin® Reader Service is committed to protecting your privacy. Our Privacy Policy is available online at www.ReaderService.com or upon request from the Harlequin Reader Service.

We make a portion of our mailing list available to reputable third parties that offer products we believe may interest you. If you prefer that we not exchange your name with third parties, or if you wish to clarify or modify your communication preferences, please visit us at www.ReaderService.com/consumerschoice or write to us at Harlequin Reader Service Preference Service, P.O. Box 9062, Buffalo, NY 14269. Include your complete name and address.

LISLPDIR13R

REQUEST YOUR FREE BOOKS!
2 FREE WHOLESOME ROMANCE NOVELS IN LARGER PRINT
PLUS 2
FREE
MYSTERY GIFTS

HEARTWARMING™

Wholesome, tender romances

YES! Please send me 2 FREE Harlequin® Heartwarming Larger-Print novels and my 2 FREE mystery gifts (gifts worth about $10). After receiving them, if I don't wish to receive any more books, I can return the shipping statement marked "cancel." If I don't cancel, I will receive 4 brand-new larger-print novels every month and be billed just $4.99 per book in the U.S. or $5.74 per book in Canada. That's a savings of at least 23% off the cover price. It's quite a bargain! Shipping and handling is just 50¢ per book in the U.S. and 75¢ per book in Canada.* I understand that accepting the 2 free books and gifts places me under no obligation to buy anything. I can always return a shipment and cancel at any time. Even if I never buy another book, the two free books and gifts are mine to keep forever.

161/361 IDN F47N

Name _____ (PLEASE PRINT)

Address _____ Apt. #

City _____ State/Prov. _____ Zip/Postal Code

Signature (if under 18, a parent or guardian must sign)

Mail to the Harlequin® Reader Service:
IN U.S.A.: P.O. Box 1867, Buffalo, NY 14240-1867
IN CANADA: P.O. Box 609, Fort Erie, Ontario L2A 5X3

* Terms and prices subject to change without notice. Prices do not include applicable taxes. Sales tax applicable in N.Y. Canadian residents will be charged applicable taxes. Offer not valid in Quebec. This offer is limited to one order per household. Not valid for current subscribers to Harlequin Heartwarming larger-print books. All orders subject to credit approval. Credit or debit balances in a customer's account(s) may be offset by any other outstanding balance owed by or to the customer. Please allow 4 to 6 weeks for delivery. Offer available while quantities last.

Your Privacy—The Harlequin® Reader Service is committed to protecting your privacy. Our Privacy Policy is available online at www.ReaderService.com or upon request from the Harlequin Reader Service.

We make a portion of our mailing list available to reputable third parties that offer products we believe may interest you. If you prefer that we not exchange your name with third parties, or if you wish to clarify or modify your communication preferences, please visit us at www.ReaderService.com/consumerchoice or write to us at Harlequin Reader Service Preference Service, P.O. Box 9062, Buffalo, NY 14269. Include your complete name and address.

HWDIR13R